★ ★ ★

Novelist **Layne Vickers Torkelson** of Albuquerque has a new career. She passed the state real estate exams and is with Preferred Properties in Corrales, and she's excited by the work. She is a graduate of Manzano High and earned a journalism degree at University of New Mexico in 1966. She was co-author of a novel, "The Balloon Affair," that *The New York Times*

Torkelson

called one of the best suspense books of 1981. She is working on a new crime novel set in Santa Fe. She is the daughter of **Arline Vickers** of Grants and has a son, **Todd**, at Alvarado School. *2/86*

★ ★ ★

To Jane Roberts —
May you always
have happy landings!

Layne
Torkelson

Delta Gamma luncheon 3/13/82

THE
BALLOON
AFFAIR

A NOVEL OF SUSPENSE

MARION MARGERY (LAYNE)

Layne Vickers Torkelson

DODD, MEAD & COMPANY
NEW YORK

Although the Albuquerque International Balloon Fiesta is an actual annual event, the characters in this novel are fictional, including all those identified by office or calling, such as city and state officials, police, etc. Any resemblance to actual persons is a coincidence.

Grateful acknowledgment to Jane Evans, former executive director, Common Cause New Mexico; Tomás Martinez, *Albuquerque Journal;* Willard Scott, Southwestern Indian Polytechnic Institute; Firearms Sgt. Bobby Vigil, New Mexico State Police; Dr. James Weston, medical examiner for the state of New Mexico; Ken Flandermeyer, M.D.; Lois Duncan, University of New Mexico; balloonists Steve Hess, Ray Bayles, and Kathy Hart; and special thanks to Hugo Cotter, attorney and friend.

1 2 3 4 5 6 7 8 9 10

Library of Congress Cataloging in Publication Data

Layne, Marion Margery.
  The balloon affair.

  I. Title.
PS3562.A956B3   813'.54   81-4903
ISBN 0-396-07951-2   AACR2

To families and teachers

ONE

The balloons bloomed suddenly—vermillion, gold, and blue—above the naked branches of the cottonwood trees. They were so low Rodriguez Riley could hear the hissing of their propane burners.

His '47 Ford pickup bumped slowly along the dirt road that wound through the bosque. He hunched over the steering wheel, his face close to the windshield, looking up. One balloon trailed a banner reading "International Hot Air Balloon Fiesta, Albuquerque, N.M."

He stopped his truck at the entrance to his driveway and stepped out on the running board. Eyes still on the balloons, Rod reached into his tin mailbox. It was empty. Strange, he thought. He bent down and peered into the box to double-check. After a month away from home there should be at least a few circulars. And he was expecting his final divorce decree. Shrugging, he tugged at his wiry red beard and climbed back into the truck. Then he noticed the two sets of tire tracks in the fresh snow that lightly powdered the ground.

"Trouble," Rod muttered. He never had visitors. His half acre down close to the Rio Grande, way back in the trees, was too hard to find.

He rammed the gearshift forward and the truck jolted

down the driveway. Without looking, he parked so the bumper of the old Ford just touched the gnarled cottonwood in front of his ramshackle adobe. A couple of chickens squawked as they fluttered out of the way, and a yellow tomcat sunning himself on the flat roof looked down to see what the racket was all about.

Rod jumped down and crossed quickly to the sagging portal, frozen brown leaves crunching under his heels. He ducked under the overhang, stopping dead. The padlock was missing and his faded blue door stood slightly ajar.

He waited cautiously in the deep shadow of the portal, head cocked, heavy shoulders hunched. Silence. He nudged the door slowly open with the toe of his boot.

The house was a shambles. His scattered papers covered the brick floor. Books had been pulled off shelves and dumped out of wooden crates. Through the doorway to the bedroom he could see the old wardrobe was empty, doors gaping. His clothes lay everywhere in jumbled piles. He grunted angrily.

The tomcat prowled into the house and rolled on a pile of undershirts. Rod eased warily through the bedroom door, but there was no one there. He relaxed his clenched fists. There were no hiding places in this small house, not even a closet, as Kate had bitterly pointed out to him so many times.

Rod picked his way through his strewn possessions back into the large room that served as his living room, study, lab, and kitchen. Slim pickings for a burglar. Kate had already cleaned him out. The last time she'd left, she'd taken the Hill Gallery furniture, the good Navajo rugs, and his sand paintings. Her legacy to him had been four bare walls, an empty bank account, bad credit, and bad wishes. The only items of value she'd overlooked were the solar balloon he had designed and the stereo equipment—and only another engineer could appreciate Rod's bare components.

Now the amplifier was smashed. Someone had deliberately pushed it from its place on the long oak table. Rod slammed his fist into the door frame. *"Cabrón!"* he growled as he lifted his bruised knuckles to his lips. Who could have done this? And what the hell for? As far as Rod could tell, nothing was missing. It wasn't burglary. Maybe kids vandalizing for kicks? Rod shook his head. Why would a kid break the padlock when he could squeeze through the small bathroom window that wouldn't ever close?

Rod shoved the front door shut. It was fairly warm in the house. The large black oil drums filled with water and stacked inside the glass south wall picked up enough heat from the sun to keep the temperature at about sixty-five degrees. The heavy shutters outside were closed during the night to trap the heat inside. Each day the cycle began again: the barrels absorbed heat during the day and radiated heat at night. The house kept time with the sun, breathing in warmth in the daylight hours, breathing it out at night. Rod loved the functional beauty of the system.

"Ugly," Kate said of his wall of giant black cans. "Looks like the city dump." That was exactly where Rod had scavenged the empty fifty-five-gallon oil drums. He carted them home on weekends in his battered pickup, returning to the dump until he had enough to assemble a free heating system in the south wall of the old adobe.

His barrel wall had created local interest, establishing him as somewhat of a solar pioneer. When the university's engineering and architectural departments asked for a guided tour, Kate's bitching about the oil drums in her living room had ceased. And the nagging began.

"Take advantage of the recognition," Kate urged. "Get a real job. Stop working for frijoles."

"You mean you want me sitting at a desk," he countered, "turning simple solar energy into a complicated process for big bucks!"

His ex-wife would never appreciate the solar installations he'd done in the small towns of northern New Mexico. Maybe a dozen schools were solar heated now, one library and four churches. None of his clients had much money, not enough to pay consultant fees, so they paid Rod to build and to teach them how to capture the sun's power, and he loved it. He loved the piney mountain roads, the tin-roofed adobe towns, working outdoors in the winelike air. Most of all he loved the challenge of scrounging materials and inventing ways to harness the sun with limited funds.

Maybe it was limited funds that drove Kate from his bed. Once, toward the end of their marriage, she'd run off to his best friend's ranch. Cliff promptly kicked her off the place. Kate just wasn't used to that treatment by a man, and it cemented her hatred of Cliff Randall. Now, evidently, she'd found someone who'd given her a warmer welcome. Rod knew she was sleeping with some minor politico and touting him to every politician she could corner. She had finally filed for divorce.

It was ironic that he, her 'discarded husband, had been invited to fly the governor in his solar balloon to help publicize the Albuquerque balloon fiesta. Rod imagined an incredulous Kate watching from the ground as he ascended with Governor Cortés in the *Sun Power*. He grinned.

The cat yowled, glaring at Rod, and began pacing impatiently along the kitchen countertop. "Take it easy, gato," Rod soothed. "I don't know where the hell your food would be in this mess." He kicked irritably at the cans and cereal boxes that had been swept off the shelves above the sink. He couldn't see any cat food, so he opened a can of Vienna sausages and set it down on the floor. The cat gave him a reproachful look and curled around the can trying to dig out its tightly packed contents.

Rod retrieved his pack from the truck and unrolled his sleeping bag. He spread it out on the bare mattress of the double bed. Then he began to clean up. All the clothes went into the open-topped Mexican basket he used as a hamper. Cans and boxes of food were replaced on the kitchen shelves as they had been before, at random. A Thrift Town assortment of plates, cups, and bowls went into the dishwasher Rod had salvaged from the city dump. He turned it on, kicked it in a practiced way, and it whined angrily into action.

While he was gathering his scattered papers, Rod discovered his missing mail. It had been opened! His empty gut contracted painfully as he picked up envelope after slashed envelope. Why would anyone want to read his mail, for Chrissakes? He pawed through the crumpled correspondence and found a schedule for the events of the balloon fiesta with a typed request that he be there promptly to lift off with the governor Saturday. There was also a short note from his friend Cliff Randall, which he read quickly:

> Since they're holding the balloon meets in February this year, don't think I'll fly the *Wind Devil*. It's too damn cold. Assume you'll be entering the *Sun Power,* anyway, now that you've finished building it.
>
> What progress with the Ójo Caliente Community Center? Give me a call when you get back from up north. I may come in for the fiesta. C.R.

Rod picked up the phone and dialed the familiar number. It had been too long since he'd seen Cliff. They'd never been comfortable together with Kate around. That was part of it, and besides, Rod's work up north took him in the opposite direction from Cliff's ranch over in Estancia Valley. He let the phone ring. No answer. Cliff was probably freezing his ass off riding around on horseback after some cows. What the hell did he mean "too cold"!

Rod scuffed through the gritty dust that always sifted over everything in his absence. There were scraps of paper and an odd button or two on the brick floor. He spotted something shiny and bent to pick it up. It was a small silver squash-blossom earring he'd once given Kate. Now where had that been all this time? He was surprised because Kate was usually careful of her good Indian jewelry. He tossed it, caught it, and put it in his shirt pocket.

He started a fire in the corner fireplace; in minutes, piñon scented the room. Hungry now, Rod rummaged up a can and ate sitting on the frayed Chimayo rug in front of the fire, shoveling diced green chile into his mouth, using pieces of tortilla as scoops.

Rod looked over the rest of his mail as he ate. His bank statement indicated he'd bounced a few checks—nothing new. He tossed it aside.

There was a letter from his mother reminding him to bring the sewing machine cam she needed when he came north again and passed through Tierra Amarilla. He skimmed her usual report on his brothers and sisters—their marriages, children, divorces, and travels. "Lupe," his mother had written about his youngest sister, "wants to drop out of school and go to Dublin. I wish you'd never started this, Rodriguez. All the rest of them sooner or later want to visit Ireland, too. It isn't as if your father had lived there. His parents left the country when he was a baby. What is it you children have to see?"

The alumni association's annual financial plea, like the twelve before it, went into the fire along with an invitation to get four marvelous books nearly free with a handkerchief-sized tote bag. He started to put a small beige note card into the fire and then retrieved it, slightly scorched. It was an engraved invitation from Ted and Moira Findley, who were celebrating the completion of the new solar addition to their house.

Rod had to hand it to Moira. She squeezed every possible drop of publicity out of anything Ted ever built. Okay, he'd go to the Findleys' party. He could probably collar Ted about a consulting job. Ted was usually glad to hire him and Rod's bank account could use a little padding. Besides, Rod thought, as he scooped the last of the canned green chile into his mouth, the Findleys' food was always great.

Rod picked up a flyer from a hardware store to toss into the fire when a long folded document slid out of it—his divorce decree. Rod thumbed curiously through the onionskin papers. He figured it would state formally what was already accomplished fact. A simple divorce. No money, no children. He got the old Ford pickup; she got the new Volvo. He got the house; she got whatever contents she wanted. "All the contents therein . . ." the decree said.

He laughed ironically, touching the silver earring in his pocket. She hadn't left much behind; she'd helped herself to most of his belongings last fall. Now, with his amplifier smashed, all he had left was the solar balloon in the lean-to attached to the back of the house.

The *Sun Power!* Was the lean-to considered part of the house? And would its contents be considered hers?

"Goddammit, no!" he roared, jumping up. The cat leaped to the mantelpiece and eyed him nervously. Rod ripped open the front door and sprinted around to the lean-to. The padlock was missing here, too. He shouldered the door aside. The lean-to was empty. His solar balloon was gone. Damn her to hell! Kate had stolen the *Sun Power!*

In the private club atop the Metropolitan Building in downtown Albuquerque, Aldo Brunalesci was paged for the phone. The maitre d' plugged it in at his table and retired discreetly.

"This is Brunalesci."

"Tige here. You told me to let you know right away what we found . . . okay to talk?"

Brunalesci looked around inconspicuously. He was early for lunch and had a table by himself in the almost deserted dining room. "Sure," he answered, staring through the plate glass at the Sandia Mountains east of the city.

"We didn't find a damn thing. We checked everywhere, even the guy's mail. If this Riley is a courier, he's not careless about it."

"You're sure? You didn't overlook anything?"

"Not a damn thing, but you didn't think he'd leave the heroin around his house, did you?"

"You can't tell with amateurs . . ."

"Only other lead is that some chick had been there before us. It looked like she took something outta the lean-to. There were tire tracks up to and back."

"A woman?"

"Well, one of them was probably a woman. There were two sets of footprints and a silver earring outside the lean-to."

Brunalesci grunted inquisitively.

"Figured it might have been his ex-wife . . . read the divorce papers. She was awarded all the contents. So I dumped the earring inside the house."

"You got time for stupid little jokes?"

"It wasn't—"

"Don't get clever. The idea of the search was to make Riley worry a lot and lead us to his boss. Now he might think it was that . . . whoever . . . ex-wife."

"I didn't—"

"Okay, okay," Brunalesci cut him off. "Just do what you're told. Don't improvise."

"Right, boss."

"Give me a call at home tonight."

"Yeah, sure thing."

Brunalesci hung up and sat staring at the mountains. He was sure Riley was the courier for whoever was siphoning heroin out of the regular syndicate pipeline. He didn't know who the moonlighter was, but he'd pretty nearly narrowed it down to someone inside the main operation. Yeah, Riley had to be the courier. But who was supplying Riley with the stuff?

Brunalesci had to find out. He was paid plenty to keep tabs on his client's narcotics operation and see that it ran smoothly.

He dialed his office. "Bernini and Brunalesci Law Offices," the receptionist answered. "Tina, I have some business to take care of. Cancel my appointments for this afternoon. Tell Mr. Bernini I'll be in tomorrow." He hung up as she was saying, "Yes, sir."

TWO

Rod hit the front door of the El Saguaro like a bull coming out of a rodeo chute and loomed there, wild eyes peering into the cavelike dimness. Two men at the end of the bar eyed him warily. One ducked his head. "Riley's got his hackles up," he muttered to his companion. "That pretty bitch he's married to must be running around again."

Rod strode past the two men, prowling the length of the room. As he neared each copper-topped table, all conversation stopped. No Kate. He retreated to the bar and sat down heavily.

The bartender handed Rod his usual Cuervo Gold and half a lime. "You seen Kate?" Rod asked. The man shook his head. "Not today," he answered. "Maybe she'll be in later."

"Rodriguez, haven't seen you for awhile," someone said at his shoulder. "How've you been?" It was Tony Lopez, who had owned the place since it was a dive with checkered linoleum floor and cheap Mexican pigskin furniture. Tony had remodeled and installed plush red carpet, gilt mirrors, and an adjoining dining room with a French chef. But the same old crowd hung out at the bar: radio and TV people, university types, and artists. Many were balloonists, and El Saguaro was their traditional gathering place during the annual hot-air balloon fiesta. Rod didn't answer Tony, who was already moving down the bar greeting customers as if he were running a stick along the rails of a fence.

In the mirrored wall back of the bar, Rod caught a glimpse of his furious face glaring out from between the lines of bottles. He was just as mad now as when he started on the search for Kate and the *Sun Power* earlier that afternoon. He'd been everywhere she might have stashed the balloon, even breaking into the garage at the house where she was living now.

Face it, he told himself, unless you get lucky, you won't see your balloon until the fiesta starts. He closed his eyes against the vivid picture this brought into his mind—Kate and the governor lifting off in the silver *Sun Power* as he stood among the spectators watching the mass ascension that opened the fiesta. Goddammit, he thought, I'll steal it back before I let that happen!

But how could you make a fast getaway in a hot-air balloon, especially under the eyes of several thousand people? Kate would never let him get away with that, not snaky Kate.

He rubbed his hand across his eyes, still fighting the hot rage. He wished that he had been born to gentle chicanos with the sorrowful patience of his grandmother, but Spanish pride and Irish rebellion carbonated his blood.

He licked the coarse salt he had put on the back of his hand and took a slug of the Cuervo, sloshing it around in his mouth before biting fiercely into the wedge of lime. The bitterness of the rind sobered him a little. He had once thought Kate might be a remedy for his volatility, but he'd mistaken her iciness for the kind of cool-headedness Cliff Randall had.

That wily bastard could keep his head in the damndest spots, Rod remembered—and he smiled as he did. Amusement cooled his anger and he began to sort out his problem in neat, almost mathematical bits.

He was positive Kate had stolen the balloon, and he had to find her to find the balloon. He had looked everywhere she might be hiding it. No luck. There was only one more place to look for Kate. She was usually on Moira Findley's guest list.

Rod glanced at the clock above the bar. The Findley party wouldn't start for two more hours.

Moira Findley checked her house for the last time to be sure everything was immaculate. She opened the linen closet and adjusted the satin ribbon that tied her stacks of matched sheets together, blue ribbon to pick up the shade in the flowered wallpaper that covered the inside of the closet. She polished a few water spots off the handpainted tile in one of the bathrooms. Perfect. She inspected herself in the mirror again. The mauve wool fell casually from her slender shoulders to the floor, a color that flattered her complexion and set off the strands of coral around her neck.

It really should be a marvelous party. The house was even lovelier with the pool enclosed by the new solar greenhouse addition. She had hated sacrificing the old garden, but the landscaped patio was elegant. Had the spotlight been turned on? Moira hurried through the pool enclosure, admiring the diffused glow of the underwater lights. Her heels clicked on the quarry tile floor. Yes, the spotlight was on, picking out the thin white birch trunks clustered just beyond the glass.

When she turned back she caught sight of her husband inventorying the bar.

"Heavens, Teddy, I've checked the liquor twice. The hors d'oeuvres have already arrived from the caterer. What tie are you wearing?" Her voice was pained.

He looked down, startled. "What's wrong with it?"

"Nothing, it's just that I had one picked out for you, that gray silk."

"Okay, okay, I'll change it."

"Señora." Moira's maid beckoned her into the kitchen. "The stew is ruined!"

"Stew? What stew? What are you talking about, Mercedes? Don't tell me the caterer delivered stew!"

"They have left the shells on the clams, señora, right in the stew!"

"Oh." Moira lifted a lid from a steam tray. "It's cioppino, Mercedes. They're supposed to be in their shells. That's the way it's made."

Mercedes's mouth drew in disapprovingly. She often criticized Moira's dishes and was especially suspicious of seafood. "It's not right . . . shells!" she hissed. With Mercedes there were always objections beforehand, but during a party service was silent and impeccable. Moira told Mercedes, "If you and Concha don't want to eat cioppino, take some steaks out of the freezer. But don't both eat at the same time. One of you should be serving the hors d'oeuvres."

Mercedes returned to the counter still shaking her head. "Clams with the shells on!" she complained to her helper Concha, who giggled. Mercedes scowled at her.

"Conca, you *boba*, stop your nonsense. This time you are to pay attention and work carefully. I will not bring you again if you are silly as last time."

Concha's simple face fell.

"The señora said you may eat a steak," Mercedes said grudgingly, and her slow-witted neighbor brightened again.

"Get it from the freezer," Mercedes said. "Eat, hurry, I need help."

"Do not be angry," Concha said softly. "I know you worry about the church, but it is God's will—"

"*No es eso*. It is not God's will. It is the will of the highway department and the stupidity of the people."

Mercedes took a large ladle from the chef's rack and began dipping clams from the cioppino, scowling as she worked. It was enough that the valley had become full of smog like that terrible place in California where her sister lived. It was enough that the farms in her little village of Alameda had been bought up, the orchards chopped down and ugly houses built; but when they insisted on tearing down the church where her mother and grandmother had been baptized, she had stayed quiet long enough.

She had been there at the meeting with the city when Luis Ruiz spoke: "It is not right to bring more cars, which the freeway will bring. It is not right to break down our church, the church that has served this town longer than most of us can remember. We pray God will help you to see how misguided you are, but if you do not see, we will place our bodies between Our Lady of Sorrows and the bulldozers."

People had applauded his speech warmly, but her granddaughter had scoffed. "Luis got that from the meeting about nuclear waste disposal," Serefina said. "I was there and heard the speech the first time it was made. Besides, when the time comes, Luis will be at the cantina, not in front of the bulldozers."

"Maybe this time we will stop them," Mercedes had answered.

Serefina had shaken her head angrily. "We should, but we will not. We make fine speeches, but no one here is prepared to risk anything."

Ah, Serefina, thought Mercedes, what has made you so bitter? Mercedes was sure it was because Serefina's mother had taken her to California when she was a young girl. There was nothing good there. Mercedes had been to visit, and she knew. Noise, dirt, and that restless ocean always sighing, sighing, sighing. It was worse than the desert wind, never at peace. And now Serefina was like that.

She had gone to the university there until a few years ago when she returned home to New Mexico. But she was strange and moody like her father, the thin, morose boy Mercedes's daughter had married. Serefina drove alone out into the desert to all the haunted Indian ruins, always digging in the earth. She said this was her work now that she was an archeologist. Mercedes thought it foolish for a young woman to drive in isolated country alone so much.

"You should have a husband," she often said to Serefina.

"And you should have children. Then you would not be always going here and there like the sea."

But Serefina, who hardly ever went to mass, had become interested in saving the church building. "It shouldn't be destroyed," she said. "They've done enough damage already."

Mercedes knew Serefina meant the remodeling, which at first looked so nice to Mercedes—the walnut paneling and carpet green and shaggy as spring grass. But since Serefina began complaining about it, images of how it looked in the old days had crept back into Mercedes's mind: The sun so white on the thick, plaster walls . . . the wide, dark floorboards . . . the altar like an angel's castle, gold and blue to the Mother of our Lord. Maybe her granddaughter was right and the old ways were better. Only we never knew it, she thought. We have always been talked out of everything.

When Mercedes had cleared the clams out of the cioppino, she tasted it. It seemed too bland, so she opened some cans of green chile, calling irritably for Concha to finish her dinner and come help get the food ready for the party.

Rod threw some change on the bar and stood up. Time to drive out to the Findleys'. He was thinking hard as he pushed through the barroom door into the flagstone foyer and bumped into someone who was coming in, a good, sturdy thump. Rod caught hold of two firm arms and looked down into a pair of frank green eyes. She was one of the best-looking blondes he'd seen in a long time.

"Sorry!" he said, dropping his hands.

She inclined her head graciously, and with a lift of an eyebrow stepped around him and went into the dining room. Somewhat stunned, Rod watched as the long, shapely legs disappeared behind the white tables and heard the maitre d' greet her, "Good evening, Mrs. Van Dressler."

"You shouldn't have let go!" a familiar voice drawled.

He whirled around. There, one shoulder leaning against the wall, Stetson on the back of his head and eyes full of the devil, was Cliff Randall.

14

"Well!" Rod laughed. "If it ain't the Marlboro man himself! How the hell are you?"

"Old Solar Bear!" Cliff boomed, slapping Rod on the back. "What's doing?"

"Hey," Rod said. "I'm just—I guess I'm just going back inside to have a drink with my compadre!"

The two of them made their way to the fireplace at the back end of the bar, greeting those people who waved at them from the small tables.

"Well," Cliff said, settling his long legs under the table and waving for the barmaid. "How's Kate?"

Rod made the motion of breaking a stick, throwing one-half to the right, the other to the left.

"You mean you finally came to your senses and got divorced?" asked Cliff.

"It's done," Rod answered, "and I have the papers to prove it. But dammit, there's one really important thing—" He broke off as the barmaid brought their drinks to the table.

She slid Rod's drink casually across the tabletop but carefully placed Cliff's glass on a paper coaster. She leaned over, the V of her bodice about two inches from Cliff's face. "Anything else, sir?" Cliff gave the cleavage a frankly appreciative glance, then raised his eyes. "Fine for now," he said smoothly. "Maybe later."

Cliff resumed as soon as she left. "You and Kate kaput? Can't say I'm sorry to hear that. I didn't think you'd ever get her out of your system."

"Out of my system, out of my house . . . only one thing left between us. She's stolen the *Sun Power*."

"She *what?*"

"She took it while I was gone up north. Got home today and found my place trashed. The shed where I keep the balloon was empty."

"She's bitch enough to have done that," Cliff said, "but I didn't think she cared that much about your balloon."

"She doesn't, but she knows I do. And she also knows I'm supposed to take the governor up Saturday at the fiesta."

15

"You are?" Cliff whistled. "How'd you manage that?"

"Fiesta officials want the governor of the sunshine state in a solar balloon. *Sun Power*'s the only solar balloon in the fiesta."

"I still don't get it."

"Kate's new lover is a small-time politico. She might think she can advance his career if she can get the governor's ear."

"And meanwhile you thought you'd get Cortés's ear to push solar energy?"

"Would I ever miss a chance? But now I can't find the balloon—or Kate—anywhere. I thought she might be here." Rod paused. "Do you know Ted Findley?"

"No."

"There's a party over there tonight, and I think Kate might just be there . . ."

"Riley," Cliff said, leaning forward, both elbows on the table, "this is not going to be one of those long academic evenings, is it?"

Lauren Brooke Madison Bradford Van Dressler finished dinner in El Saguaro's dining room with coffee, deciding against the mousse. She pushed her fingers through her honey-colored hair and gazed around, looking for the gorgeous cowboy she'd been eyeing when she collided with that redheaded mountain in the entry. Evidently he had gone into the bar instead of the dining room.

She smoked idly, her bottle-green eyes narrowed against the smoke. No one remotely interesting . . . mostly husbands of clients. And if there was one policy sacred to Lauren Van Dressler, it was: don't touch the clients' husbands.

She wondered whether to go to the Findleys' party. Why not? The drinks would be good, and besides, it would be good for business. Maybe she even owed it to Moira Findley, who never failed to give the Enchanted Door Beauty Ranch a plug, telling everyone who said, "How marvelous you're looking!" that it was Lauren who kept her looking that way—always adding a little ingenuously that Teddy had designed the Enchanted Door.

16

But then, thought Lauren, it works. Moira's social contacts keep customers flocking to the Door. And I turn them over to the dietitians, masseuses, and hairdressers and send them away . . . well, at least repaired a little. I was right about the business potential in this city and oh, do they need me! All of them, fat, skinny, or just drab.

Lauren reached for her wallet to pay the check and it fell open to pictures of the three men with whom she had spent ten years of her life trying to find legal bliss.

Chuck Madison's publicity picture. They'd eloped to New York City the night of their graduation from the Brattleboro, Vermont, high school. He'd tried to work as an actor; she'd gotten a job as receptionist at the Elizabeth Arden Salon. What a match they had been for each other sexually. But then, it turned out Chuck was a match for anyone, sexually.

The second time she'd gone for money. She'd met Harry Bradford in the lobby of the Waldorf-Astoria. He was in New York on a business trip, selling South American gems. Those were comfortable years. She thought of the spacious house in Ipanema with its clipped hedges and capable servants, the sound of lazy palm trees rattling in the breeze from the sea. And she sighed. If Harry was a match for *anybody* sexually, she'd never discovered it.

Husband number three, pictured so serious here in his uniform, had been the naval attaché at the American embassy. When he was transferred to Hawaii she went with him, carrying only a bag of bikinis and a coffee can full of gemstones.

She wasn't sure why she'd left him, too. Perhaps it was the torpor of lush, perpetual summer in an island paradise, or the monotony of his vigorous but uninspired lovemaking. In any case, she'd bailed out.

When Lauren docked in San Francisco, she thumbed her way east on US-66. Liabilities: three faded bikinis. Assets: a coffee can full of gems.

In Albuquerque she found an overgrown boom town spreading like an amoeba, a city with two universities, its own civic opera and symphony, a Junior League, a couple of country clubs—and here, she quickly saw, was a clientele salivating for a really elegant beauty spa. And she had been right. Her investment was paying off handsomely.

She stubbed out her cigarette, tossed a large bill on the table, and scooping up her fox-lined trench coat, left the dining room trailing expensive perfume.

Theodore Findley found the gray tie on his dresser. He looked at the clock. Good, he could see part of the evening news before the party. He switched on the TV set in the wall beside his mirror and glanced at the screen hoping to catch the footage shot that afternoon of his solar addition. The news director had told Moira he couldn't promise which evening the film would be shown, but Moira managed to get almost every one of Ted's projects on the news since his first solar building had been featured in *Progressive Architecture*. He had built his reputation on solar design. Thank God for Rodriguez Riley's technical expertise.

Ted turned up the volume.

And at the top of the news, governors from the border states ended their three-day conference in Austin with a pledge to crack down on drug smuggling across the Mexican border. Governor Cortés will return to New Mexico in time to open the balloon festival Saturday morning. Hundreds of balloonists from all over the world will participate in the week-long international balloon fiesta that begins with the mass ascension Saturday at eight A.M. Other dignitaries who will take part in the inaugural lift-off include Lieutenant Governor Betty Morrison, U.S. Senator George Claridge, City Commissioner Allan Blake, and Archbishop Grignard.

Ted turned his collar up and draped the tie loosely around his neck. He glanced back at the screen.

In Santa Fe, the state legislature ended its long session today by passing more than one hundred bills, voting in blocks of five and ten bills at a time. . . .

Dammit, why wouldn't this tie do what he wanted it to do? He jerked at the fine fabric, concentrating on his image in the mirror. Suddenly he became aware of what the announcer was saying.

. . . the so-called Sunshine Tax bill carried an emergency clause and was signed into law by Lieutenant Governor Betty Morrison, acting in the governor's absence. The controversial law will tax all properties that have solar collectors of any kind.

Ted Findley stood open-mouthed before the television, incredulity setting the lines of his face. That damned tax passed! Where in hell was the A.I.A. lobby? He rushed into the bedroom and picked up the extension, dialing furiously. He got a busy signal. Moira came into the bedroom.

"Teddy, what *are* you doing?"

"The energy tax. . ." he began, listening helplessly as the busy signal continued. "The damned energy tax passed!" he said, slamming down the phone.

"What?"

"A tax on solar energy just went through the legislature and was signed by the lieutenant governor—"

"Teddy, please don't shout."

"For Christ's sake, Moira, didn't you hear what I said?"

"Yes, dear, an energy tax passed . . ."

"How *can* you be so dense? They're taxing solar energy. My practice will fall apart—"

"Now, darling, people may fuss, but they always pay taxes. I don't see why they'll object any more to paying taxes on solar energy than they do on gas or electricity."

Findley ran his finger around under his collar, loosening his tie. Moira tightened it, patting it into place.

"People will pay tax on gas and electricity because they know it costs money to deliver them," he explained wearily. "So they figure that as part of their operating costs. But goddammit, sunshine's supposed to be free." He shrugged off her patting hands.

"Theodore," Moira said, drawing herself up in a way that was well known to the boards of a number of museums, "I don't think this is an issue it is appropriate to consider now. We have guests arriving in a few minutes."

"For God's sake—"

She avoided looking at him. "Please, dear, don't ruin our party with politics." Moira permitted her eyes to brim with tears, a habit that had been engaging when she was nineteen, but now made her look rheumy eyed.

"All right, all right." Ted stormed out of the bedroom. Moira took a tissue from the bedside stand and carefully blotted the moisture from her lower lids. She would have to monitor Teddy's circulation among their guests; otherwise he'd get off in a corner and start on this tax thing. She looked in the mirror, adjusted a curl with an enameled fingernail, smiled at her reflection, and followed her husband into the living room.

Her eyes were drawn to one empty niche. The large antique pot Valencio Loretto had promised to deliver was supposed to be displayed there tonight. Her lips tightened. Valencio was so undependable! Teddy would have said he was running on Indian time again. The niche could not possibly be left empty. She snatched a trailing green plant from a low table. "There, that'll have to do, I suppose."

There were cars parked along the street for blocks when Joe Loretto and his uncle Valencio drove up to the Findleys' house in Joe's new Chevy pickup. Joe refused to go in. He parked the truck and folded his arms. His uncle wasted no time arguing but got out of the truck carefully, holding the large black-and-white pot, chipped and faded, decorated with ancient designs. Before he closed the door he said to Joe, "They got some good food in there." Joe just scowled. He hated going with his uncle when he sold pottery. The suckers wanted to buy antique Indian pottery so bad you could practically sell plastic copies.

Valencio's were clay, though, cleverly aged. Joe's sister made them. She had studied to be a dental technician, but had discovered her skill enabled her to turn out two or three large "antique" pots a month.

"I don't know why you do it," Joe had said to her, disgusted.

"I like the income," she replied placidly. "It beats six bucks an hour all to hell."

"Why do you have to play crazy old Indian?" Joe had asked his uncle. "They laugh at you."

"Maybe white man naturally happy" was all Valencio had said, exaggerating his Tewa accent.

Once, when Joe had gone with his uncle to do yard work for the Findleys, Mrs. Findley had said, "Valencio, you told me a red headband is for a married man and a green one is for a single man, but I see your nephew is wearing a yellow headband. What does that mean?"

"Crazy," Valencio had answered solemnly. "Crazy spirits speak to him."

Mrs. Findley had giggled nervously. "I see. Is he . . . ah. . .?"

"Only at night."

"Well . . . ah . . . imagine!" she'd said, and gone into the house. Joe's uncle went on raking the yard.

"Why'd you lie?" Joe asked furiously. "Why make up a stupid story like that?"

"Why not?" Valencio had countered. "Mrs. Findley wants to know all about our customs, so I give her some customs to tell her friends. *Indian lore,*" Valencio grunted, winking at Joe.

"I don't know why I hang around you," Joe said disgustedly.

"You're learning the business," Valencio said calmly, continuing his raking.

"What business?"

"To be an Indian."

"I *am* an Indian."

"No. Wearing long hair tied up the old way and making insults to the government is not what it takes."

"My blood makes me an Indian."

"Your blood makes you nothing. Brains is what makes you an Indian—and you got none!"

"I got plenty. I don't have to be an Uncle Tonto."

"How much money you make?" Valencio asked him. "How much you figure you make a year?"

"You know I work for the Native American Movement as a volunteer!"

"How about the adobe yard?"

"Scraping and turning blocks?" Joe was disdainful. "That's just part time."

"How much does it pay you?" Valencio persisted. "How much money to break your ass?"

Joe scowled silently.

"Peanuts!" Valencio said. "Because you think like white man. I think Indian—adapt. I sell pottery. I tell customs. Good old Valencio. I make in one day what you make in two weeks. Because you all the time fighting. You not yet learn—there's more of them than us. But they are like the buffalo. Give us all we need to live if hunted carefully."

Joe looked suspiciously at his uncle. Valencio was likely to be putting him on. Valencio resumed raking without saying more.

When they went back to the truck after his uncle had finished, Joe said, "I don't know why I cart you around."

"Because I got no car."

"You got your goddam Porsche, you crazy old man."

"Not Indian car."

"Well, I'm gonna stop carrying you."

Valencio didn't reply.

And here, thought Joe, watching his uncle's toe-first walk across the Findleys' lighted terrace, I am again.

A few minutes after Valencio had carried the pot into the house, an old '47 Ford pickup parked in front of Joe, and he watched two men get out.

"No longer than half an hour, Cliff," the large bearded one said. "I just want to see if Kate's here. Then we'll go back to Tony's and tie one on."

The other man wore a Stetson and sheepskin coat. "My, oh, my," he said, suddenly pointing at a white Bentley. "I do believe that's the car that fine-looking blonde was driving."

"Huh?"

"You know, the leggy one you bumped into at El Saguaro."

"Yeah, yeah."

"Well, old buddy," the cowboy said, adjusting his Stetson, "let's go to the party."

The two of them went up the walk without seeing Joe sitting in his parked truck. He decided they'd already had a few drinks. He looked at his watch. Valencio had been gone about five minutes. I'll give the old bastard an hour, he thought, and he settled down so the traditional knot of hair at the nape of his neck cushioned his head against the back of the seat.

When Lt. Bernardo Martinez checked his patrol car in for the night at state trooper headquarters in Santa Fe, he found a message to call a number in Albuquerque. He stuffed the note in his shirt pocket and went off duty. On the drive to his house he stopped his Audi at the Free Fraser Pharmacy and bought some aspirin, asking for his change in dimes, nickels, and quarters. He called from a pay phone.

The phone was answered on the first ring. "Rick," he said, "this is Bernie."

"The '47 Ford truck is back in town," Rick told him.

"*Bueno.*"

"That guy makes me nervous."

"Riley?" Bernardo asked. "Why?"

"You claim he don't have no idea he's carryin' the stuff on his truck. But today he's been actin' like he knows somethin' . . . or he's just plain crazy."

"What's that supposed to mean?"

"He come into town this mornin'. We spotted him turnin'

on the river road. Then, about half an hour later, he runs out back to his shed and then he hops in the truck and takes off like a madman. He went all the hell over the city . . . breakin' into houses, pushin' past people, like he was lookin' for somebody."

"Whaddya mean?"

"I think Riley's on to us. He's huntin' someone or some *thing*."

"How could he be on to us? He doesn't know he's being used as a courier. He couldn't even find the stuff accidentally up under those high fenders. It's all covered with mud under there, a guy would have to know what to look for even if he looked right at it. Nah, he doesn't know." Bernie paused. "Where is the truck now?"

"It's outside this big place off Rio Grande Boulevard . . . big fancy house . . . looks like they got a party goin' on."

"Well, get the smack on that truck! They're expecting delivery in Denver next week. We don't want to miss Riley's trip up north this time. Do it now while he's busy and there are some people around making noise."

"But with this much stuff . . . Jesus, Bernie, if we get caught—"

"Listen, I thought you and your cousin were smart kids. If not, maybe I should find somebody else who'd like the money."

"No! No, Bernie . . . we'll take care of it."

"*Bueno*. If it gets there on schedule, maybe I'll have a little bonus for you."

"Sure. Yeah. Okay, Bernie."

Bernardo hung up the phone and rummaged in his pocket for the aspirin box. He ate two aspirins dry, wincing. This would have to be the last time for Rick. The kid was jumpy as a tick around sheep dip. And this might be Riley's last run, too. The attorney general's investigators were monitoring incoming traffic to that part of the state. They'd soon catch on that the drug often showed up in the northern villages a day

24

or two after Riley hit town. Sooner or later they were bound to search his truck. Professionals would know the right places to look. Well, that'd be Riley's problem.

His own problems were bigger. He'd gotten used to the cash. At first he had promised himself it would only be one moonlight run, but that one had paid off so well, he'd done another . . . then another. He might have gotten away with one, even if his boss caught on that he'd shorted the regular shipments to run his own operation. It was the quantities he'd ripped off; they'd never overlook that. And that damn Brunalesci was smart. Bernie's boss, State Security Chief Hans Daggett, had told him yesterday that Brunalesci suspected someone was stealing from the syndicate pipeline. So far no one knew he, Bernie, was the leak. Still, maybe he ought to forget this run. The risk was accelerating.

THREE

The heavy crystal glasses, most of them still full of ice, caught the light in the deserted living room and threw back as many sparks as a flock of stars. Prismlike designs patterned the white plastered walls and the dark wood ceiling, splashed on the chrome of the low-slung chairs, and speckled the glass coffee table with small patches of sparkle.

Moira stood staring at the kaleidoscopic effect. Her party had undeniably flopped. Most of the guests seemed as upset as Teddy by the solar energy tax . . . what had they called it? The sunshine tax. God, she'd heard enough on that subject to last her for the rest of her life! You'd have thought they were going to start a revolution. Taxes were taxes . . . if not this one, then there'd be another.

She certainly didn't think this sunshine tax was important enough to have disrupted her entire housewarming. She was disgusted with them all, especially Lauren Van Dressler, who never took an interest in politics. She was sure that Lauren had jumped into the discussion only because that big, macho cowboy friend of Riley's had been involved. Maybe Lauren was reaching that age where women get desperate. That's what happens, Moira thought smugly, when you just divorce anytime you feel like it.

She could hear voices coming from the kitchen. They were still at it, the diehards who hung around after the main party had withered away. Sighing, she collected a few glasses as an excuse to go in without seeming purely curious.

She marched briskly into the kitchen intending to pointedly ignore Teddy, who'd behaved terribly, but he didn't even notice she'd entered the room. He was at the butcher-block island talking intently with Riley and his friend . . . Mr. Clifford? . . . Oh, what was his name . . . the cowboy. And there, sure enough, was Lauren perched on the counter beside them.

Raising her chin angrily, Moira started toward the pantry and jumped as she passed the breakfast room. There in the dark alcove was Valencio, just sitting quietly, listening. She frowned at him, but he didn't look at her. She'd have to make it clear to him later that there were certain proprieties. She supposed all Indians were this way—they didn't know how to take social hints. He had no sense, anyway, to bring the pottery to sell to her during the party. She pushed irritably through the pantry door.

Mercedes and Concha were putting food away and loading the dishwasher. Moira thrust the glasses into Concha's hands and stalked through the pantry. Suddenly she picked up a large bowl and held it accusingly toward Mercedes. It was full of clams. "Mercedes," Moira demanded, "what are these?"

Mercedes came unwillingly to look into the bowl. "Clams," she admitted, "my cat likes them."

Moira opened her mouth to protest, but shut it helplessly. "Then what," she finally asked, "did my guests eat?"

"Everything but the clams," Concha offered helpfully. "When the caterer's food was gone, I take the carne adovada from the freezer and heat it in the microswave. They eat that, too."

Moira moaned, but Mercedes looked so fierce and was so silent, she hurried back into the kitchen.

"Of course they think they can get away with it," Rod was

saying. "Every legislative body in this country is sure we'll keep right on taking it, and if not smiling, at least not kicking up too much of a fuss."

Ted shook his head morosely. "I just can't believe no one recognized the implications of this tax before it was passed." He stood up and reached for a bottle. "If someone had, they'd have seen what the state's really doing is slapping us with a damned expensive property tax." He poured out a glass of Scotch. "You'd think the press would have been all over it . . ."

"Can't count on the press, Ted." Rod held out his glass for a refill. "Too bad some sharp reporter didn't add two and two together and figure the uranium interests had to do something like this eventually to hinder solar energy development."

"Really," said Lauren, "you sound like you think someone's deliberately fighting solar power."

"Yeah," Ted said, "why would anyone do a thing like that? Why would a multibillion-dollar industry try to stop the population of the good old U.S.A. from using power that can't be monopolized? Should the fact that there's no need to build solar reactors upset them?"

"Come on, Ted," Lauren said. "You're spouting off like the environmentalists. They're probably right, but they got so wrapped up in their own rhetoric, they didn't even see this sunshine tax coming."

"It came pretty fast," Cliff said. "No news coverage before the fact, no sit-ins by the environmentalists, no filibusters."

The room grew silent except for the occasional tinkling of ice cubes. Cliff and Lauren studied their drinks as if reading tea leaves. Rod hunched over the butcher-block island, his hand moving furiously over a small telephone pad, filling the paper with balloon shapes. Moira stood awkwardly, hands clasped before her.

"So nobody was watching," Rod broke the silence, "including us."

Lauren reached for the bottle Ted had set on the counter and poured herself Scotch neat. "You know," she mused, "times have changed. When I was growing up in New England, we always had these town meetings." She tasted her drink and, gesturing with it, went on. "Everyone attended, even the kids. Everyone had to have his say. No one could have foisted anything like this sunshine tax over on those people. Everyone knew what was going on and wanted to have a voice in it. Remember, that's the part of the country that threw the Boston Tea Party."

"The Boston Tea Party," Moira recited, "was the work of a few agitators and—"

"You sound like a royalist," Cliff laughed.

"I'm a Republican," Moira said stiffly. Everyone laughed but Moira, who'd spoken quickly without thinking. Ted laughed the loudest, waving the Scotch bottle recklessly.

"Teddy!" Moira cried, as he narrowly missed a hanging plant.

"Don't call me Teddy," he said between his teeth.

"I've never seen you like this," Moira said coldly. "And I'm sure we can manage a tax!"

"Moira," Lauren said in a firm voice, "I think what's bothering Ted is the way the tax will affect his business. People interested in using solar power come to Ted. And when the economic realities of this tax hit, well, no one's going to want to use solar energy. You see?"

"Now, surely, it's not all that desperate," Moira began in a superior tone. "Teddy—Ted's a great designer. We'll attract—he'll attract—other clients. It's not that bad." Without looking at her, Ted poured himself another drink.

"It *is* that bad," Rod said. "After a while, when people forget the reason no one uses solar power is because of the heavy taxation, you watch—they'll start saying nuclear power is our only alternative. No one can make money off sunshine."

"My God," Moira said, "you're surely not going to start some sophomoric argument against nuclear power?"

"I could," Rod said wearily, "but I'm not. This looks like some legislation that was aimed and timed very carefully."

"Then it's a clumsy ploy," Lauren argued. "I wouldn't be surprised to see this tax tested in the courts."

"Sure, but how many years can it be dragged out?" Rod asked.

"Well, dammit, there are other ways," Lauren persisted. "The governor could call a special session of the legislature—"

"Could—*if* he was here and *if* he wanted to," Cliff replied.

"That's right," Moira said. "Remember, Governor Cortés left while the legislature was in session. Maybe he knew all about the sunshine tax and planned it this way. Lieutenant Governor Morrison signed it, so he'll escape the blame."

Lauren's eyes narrowed. "Moira does have a point. Doesn't it seem a bit coincidental that the bill carried an emergency clause so it would be signed into law right away—before Cortés theoretically could be expected to veto it?"

"No," Rod said, shaking his head. "That's off by miles. Just isn't Cortés's style. This conference in Texas has been planned for a long time. The governor's serious about stopping narcotics traffic through the state. He grew up poor in northern New Mexico and saw what heroin has done to the kids up there. He hates it. And, besides, he's always favored solar energy development."

"Right," Cliff agreed. "This is a quick and dirty move by someone else, someone who knows the old political two-step. Looks like the lieutenant governor was in touch with someone who made her an offer she couldn't refuse."

"Such as?" Moira asked.

"Such as running for governor next term, campaign funds to be supplied by *friends* . . . not to mention lots of support and coverage as the first woman governor of New Mexico. What a coup she's pulled off!"

Suddenly a strange look crossed Cliff's face. He stood up, turned his chair around with one hand, set it back down, and straddled it. His eyes looked mischievous, Moira thought, and a crafty grin curved his mouth. His eyes met Rod's.

"You've got to get your balloon back from Kate, my friend," Cliff said. "It's the only *patriotic* thing to do."

"My balloon?" Rod was momentarily puzzled. "The *Sun Power?*" Then Moira saw the same strange expression steal over Rod's face, quickly followed by a look of complete understanding. The corners of his mouth twitched into a smile. "Ah, yes, my *balloon*," Rod sighed.

"What are you two talking about?" she asked irritably.

Cliff turned to her. "Rod made this solar balloon, see, and the fiesta committee's asked him to take the governor up on Saturday. You know, a publicity thing—"

"Soooo," Lauren drew out huskily, "Rod and the governor will be together. . ." She gestured at the ceiling.

Cliff reached up and pulled her arm down until it pointed to the floor.

"There's a hitch," he said. "Rod's ex-wife has the balloon. We have to . . . uh . . . get it back so Rod can fly Cortés."

Lauren's hand brushed the air in an impatient gesture. "So you get the balloon back and fly Cortés Saturday. When you're up in the air with him, you'd still have to convince him to call a special session."

"Yep," Cliff said agreeably, "but that ain't the only way to skin this cat!"

"Very folksy," Lauren commented drily. "What do you mean?"

"Well," Rod began, "if you've got the governor up in the air and you refuse to bring him down until—"

"That's kidnapping!" Moira gasped.

"Well, now, little lady," Cliff said easily, "not exactly kidnapping. We won't harm anyone or ask for ransom. Just buying a little publicity, you might say. Give the news media time to pick it up. Story'd probably make the wire services. Raise a little ruckus—"

"Boston Tea Party West!" Lauren whistled.

Rod grabbed her and hugged her.

"Here," Cliff said, prying Rod's arms away. "Let me do that!" He pulled Lauren to him and kissed her.

Moira frowned slightly. "Are you saying this hijacking—well, skyjacking—is to get the voters to—"

"Insist on a special session to repeal the tax," Cliff finished for her.

"Well." Lauren stood up and put her arm around Cliff's shoulders. "Why play for small stakes? As I recall, a city commissioner, a U.S. senator—and did I hear it was the archbishop?—are also going up in balloons to open the fiesta."

"You're my kind of woman, Lauren," Cliff said, and kissed her again. Lasciviously, Moira thought.

"Don't forget the looten't governor," Ted volunteered. "She'll be there, too."

"The archbishop?" Cliff asked. "Should we take him?"

"Church and state . . . whoever we can get," Rod said. "Sure, take him!"

Moira thought she heard the pantry door creak. Could Mercedes be eavesdropping? But when she looked, she could see nothing. And Valencio seemed to have disappeared from the breakfast alcove. Moira turned back, distressed to see Ted pouring himself another drink. He ought to stop. Things were getting out of hand.

"There's just one detail that bothers me," Lauren said. "How can we hijack that many balloons?"

"Only one way," Cliff said. "We'd have to knock out each pilot before lift-off."

"Knock out each pilot!" Moira shrieked. "I thought you said you weren't going to hurt anybody!"

Rod tugged at his beard. "We might have to do something like that. I mean, you can't pull a gun and make a fast getaway in a balloon, for Chrissakes."

"Well, how in hell are we gonna get rid of the pilots then?" Lauren asked.

The pantry door creaked open.

"Needles," said a quiet voice. "Give them shots."

They all looked toward the pantry door where Mercedes stood, head high, hands clasped demurely in front of her dotted Swiss party apron.

"Mercedes," Moira gasped, "have you been listening to this?"

Mercedes ignored her, dark eyes fastened on Rod's face. "*Les damos un shot*," she repeated.

"Hypodermics," Rod mused. "Sure . . . exactly the way to do it. But how?" Rod let the question hang in the air.

"Our altar society helps the nurses at the hospital. We all learn to give the shots. One *piquito* and they sleep like this." She snapped her fingers to illustrate. "Later they wake up okay."

Everyone watched her solemnly. She walked closer to Rod.

"But could we get the drug?" he asked.

"I could. I have a friend. She works in the hospital. My friend could get it."

"But would she, knowing she could go to jail if she were caught?"

Mercedes nodded. "*Sí*, I am . . . she, my friend, that is, *she* is very careful. And it is for a good cause. She will get the drug."

"Mercedes," Moira said, shocked. "Don't tell me you're interested in the sunshine tax?"

Mercedes shook her head briefly.

"Then why?" asked Rod. "*Por qué?*"

"I do it if you will let me talk to the archbishop. Only he can save our church."

"I'll get you to the archbishop," Rod promised.

"*Gracias*." Mercedes smiled. "And for this my friends and I will do the needles."

"Your friends?"

"*Sí*, the Altar Society of Our Lady of Sorrows. It is for a good cause."

"An altar society?" Cliff asked, his voice breaking a little.

"*Sí*," Mercedes told him. "We will do it. We do volunteer work and drive everywhere in our bus. I am sure Father Paul will let us have the bus on Saturday. I will tell him we are working to save our church. *Eso es verdad*, is truth, no?"

Moira saw that Cliff's arms were folded, his head bowed. One hand covered his face.

"Er . . ." Rod started, "I guess that would be all right." He turned to get Cliff's approval and saw his friend's shoulders jiggling slightly.

Mercedes looked at Cliff. "You think it's funny, but you will see—we have stingers."

At that Cliff burst out laughing, which made Rod laugh too, and then Mercedes joined them momentarily. "But remember," she cautioned, "I do this only if I can talk to the archbishop."

"*Promeso*," Rod said solemnly.

"Mercedes," Moira said, "I can't let you do this. It's crazy. I thought it was just a joke but you're all really serious about this, aren't you?"

"You bet!" Ted announced in a loud voice.

"Oh, no, Teddy," Moira said, shaking her head, "you're out of your mind if you think I'm going to—"

"Not you," Ted said with a grandiose drunken gesture. Then, pointing to himself, he said, "Bu' I am."

Moira turned angrily on Mercedes. "You can go home now, Mercedes," she said stiffly. "You and Concha can leave now."

"Concha is gone already," Mercedes told her serenely. "My granddaughter will come for me on her way home." Mercedes headed back to the pantry.

"Well then," Lauren said briskly, "you got your needles, and you got your hijackees. But who's going to fly all these balloons?"

"Who knows how to fly a balloon?" Cliff asked.

Ted shook his head solemnly with great control, Lauren shook her head quickly, and Moira stared at Cliff wide-eyed.

"So Rod and I'll teach you," Cliff said.

"B-b-but people will see you knock the pilots out," Moira protested. "How do you expect to get away with it?"

"In that crowd, with all that confusion, no one will even notice," Cliff said. "If they do, there'll only be one downed pilot where they are. They'll never make a connection. Think the pilot fainted or something."

"If everything goes smoothly," Rod said.

"Teddy and I have been on ground crews—chase crews—I'd have noticed if the pilot of my balloon was unconscious."

"Right . . . the chase crews," Rod said. "We gotta do something to distract them."

"A bubble dance," Lauren volunteered. Then she sat up and said brightly, "No, wait a minute. I've got it! Champagne! Give them some free champagne—yes! Right! A free champagne breakfast just before launch—er, lift-off."

"That would do it," Cliff said. "Yep, I'm getting to like your mind." He kissed Lauren on the neck and whispered something in her ear.

"Well, this has gone far enough!" Moira cried. "I'm not listening to another word of it. I'm not going along with you and my husband isn't either!"

Ted got unsteadily to his feet. "Am," he said. "M'ra, lemme tell you s'mping." He pointed at her, then stood mute.

"He's run down," Lauren whispered to Cliff.

Cliff said, "We could go out to my ranch in Estancia Valley and tomorrow Rod and I can teach you to fly."

"In just one day?" Lauren asked.

"Sure," Cliff said.

"Am," Ted said again.

"Sure, you're going, Ted," Cliff said.

"Ranch." Ted nodded carefully.

"What about you, Mercedes?" Cliff called. "Do you want to come out to my ranch with us now?"

"My granddaughter will bring me to your ranch tomorrow morning," said Mercedes quietly. She came out of the pantry wearing a dark cloth coat, a black shawl over her head.

"I don't know—" Rod protested.

"Perfect," Cliff said. He picked up the telephone pad, tore off Rod's page of doodled balloons and started sketching. "Look," he said. "My ranch is called the Last Frontier. There's a sign on the highway. Here, I'll draw you a map."

There was a brisk knock at the kitchen door. Mercedes

opened it and a tall black-eyed young woman entered. "My granddaughter, Serefina," Mercedes said.

"Good evening." Serefina smiled. Her dark hair was twisted into a heavy chignon. She wore a long ice-blue silk coat and no jewelry except a pair of turquoise stud earrings. Moira noticed Lauren seemed impressed by her understated elegance.

"Have you been waiting long?" Serefina asked.

Mercedes shook her head. "No, you are here at the right time. Come, there are some things I want to take home, some scraps for the cat and . . . come." Mercedes led the way to the pantry.

Cliff snapped his fingers in front of Rod's face. "She's gone now," he teased. Rod jerked around red-faced. "Class," Cliff said quietly. "But back to the hijack." He smiled at Rod. "We've left out one important thing. A place to come down. We aren't going to be able to stay aloft long enough to get a media blitz going. We need a hideout. Someplace within thirty miles that's isolated. Got any ideas?"

Moira saw that Rod's face was still flushed. Why, Rod's shy with her, she thought. Imagine!

Suddenly Serefina stalked out of the pantry and confronted Rod, leaning toward him and slamming down the bowl of clams on the butcher-block island.

"*Pendejo*! You idiot! What do you think you're doing, getting my grandmother involved in this insane scheme? How dare you take advantage of an old woman!"

Rod's eyes were wide with shock. "I—w—w—we—" he stammered.

"People like you should be put away!"

"Shhh . . . *cálmate, déjame explicar*," Mercedes began, hurrying to Serefina's side.

"Oh, let's go home," Serefina said. She whirled and strode past the breakfast alcove, her high heels as loud as gunshots on the tile floor. Instantly there was a bloodcurdling yelp as Serefina jumped back.

"Valencio!" Moira exclaimed, peering under the breakfast table. "How long have you been there?"

"Too long," the old Indian muttered, holding his foot and scowling at Serefina.

Serefina tossed her head, her nostrils flaring.

"You . . . er, ah . . . you forgot your clams," Rod said, picking up the heavy bowl. It tilted as he held it toward her. Clams spilled out, their hard shells ricochetting off the smooth wooden counter. They spun across the kitchen, and to Rod's horror, several splattered on the front of Serefina's blue silk coat.

Rod cringed as Serefina turned without a word and stared at him disdainfully. In complete silence she stalked out. Her grandmother followed, murmuring "mañana" to Cliff as she passed him.

Cliff put his hands in his pockets and shrugged. "I think she likes you."

Rod threw a clam at him. "Oh, swell, now that everything's falling into place, we've got to scratch it," he said bitterly. "Because of that . . . woman!" He kicked another clam, which skittered across the floor.

Cliff rubbed his ear. "Maybe," he said slowly.

"No maybe, you heard her! She's mad and she's liable to do whatever she can to stop us."

Moira smiled smugly. Everyone was quiet.

Mercedes came back into the kitchen. "I do not want you to worry," she said to Rod. "Serefina has promised to listen to me. And she has promised she will do nothing until she hears all that I have to say."

"And then?" Rod asked.

"By then she will join us."

"Join us?"

"*Ciertamente*. She also fights the atom-bomb people."

"The who?"

"Oh, the uranium companies." Cliff laughed.

"*Sí*," Mercedes assured him. "She goes to the meetings to

stop the waste disposal. Do not worry. She will help. You will see." Mercedes touched Rod's hand lightly and left the kitchen.

"Cliff," asked Rod, "do you think Mercedes knows what she's talking about?"

"I'd bet my ranch on it," Cliff said. "She put it all together from what she heard us talking about tonight. Oh, yes, indeedy, I would bet Mercedes knows what she's about. And I'd say Serefina will fly with us when her grandmother gets done talking."

"Well," Rod shrugged, "anyway, we don't know where we could land."

Abruptly a guttural voice said, "Tipi village."

"Huh?"

Valencio spoke out of the gloom beneath the table. "Take people to tipi village. Good place to hide governor."

"You mean that old movie set out near the reservation?" Cliff asked. The old man nodded once, sharply.

"Not a bad idea," Rod said. "So obvious, no one would think to look there."

"Okay," Cliff yawned, "let's all go out to my ranch and get some sleep. We can hash this over tomorrow."

"Go," Ted said instantly.

Cliff took Lauren's arm. "You ride with me. Let Rod bring the Findleys in your car."

"Okay," Lauren agreed. "Here," she said, lightly tossing her keycase to Rod.

"What about you, chief?" Cliff asked Valencio.

"My nephew drives me. We will come in his truck."

"Coming, Moira?"

"*Am!*" said Ted.

"I suppose so," Moira said grudgingly through pursed lips. "I'll be right with you." She went to the bedroom to get her overnight case.

"Okay," Cliff called, rubbing his hands together. "Let's get this tea party under way!"

Moira shuddered as she dumped a bottle of Alka-Seltzer into her purse for Teddy in the morning.

Bernardo's wife, Angie, lay on the den couch snoring softly, plump legs peeking out of lavender chiffon ruffles. Bernie sat staring at the test pattern. Christ, it was after three in the morning. Why in hell hadn't Rick called? Where was the stupid freak? Probably out somewhere getting high.

Angie snorted gently and after a few swallows resumed her faint snoring. Bernie rubbed the bridge of his nose. When he'd come home, she'd greeted him at the door with a marguerita. He knew from the lavender peignoir that she wanted to make love. "Ah, geez, I'm bushed, Angie," he'd pleaded, fending off her insistent hands. But he hadn't been able to offend her. And, as it turned out, she wouldn't be put off.

He picked up the phone and dialed the number in Albu-querque again. It rang unanswered. *"Pendejo,"* he cursed, slamming the phone down. Then he threw a worried look over his shoulder at Angie on the couch. He knew if he woke her she'd want it again.

Wearily, he got out of the La-Z-Boy, the Naugahyde pulling painfully away from his bare skin. Slowly, he stooped and retrieved his orange Jockey shorts, and, balancing awkwardly on one leg and then the other, got them on. He was cold, so he padded into the bedroom for a robe. The phone gave a convulsive ting, getting ready to ring. He pounced on the extension beside the bed before it could arouse the ravenous Angie.

"Yeah?" he growled into it.

"Bernie?" A hoarse whisper identified Wilfred, Rick's cousin.

"Yeah," Bernie snapped. "Where's Rick?"

"Oh, he's okay. The lawyer said he'll be out in half an hour."

"Out!" Bernie yelped, then remembering Angie, lowered

his voice. "Whadda ya mean out? Out of where?" A steady hammering in the back of his head told him his headache was resuming double time.

"R-R-Rick's okay now, Bernie. The lawyer said they can't do nothing. The lawyer has to talk to him, that's all, then Rick'll be back on the street again. I'm gonna wait here until he's out and then we'll just go on home."

"Where the hell," asked Bernie, speaking slowly between his teeth, "is Rick?"

"I'm telling you—"

"Just answer my question," Bernie said, enunciating his words carefully. "*Now*."

He heard a long sigh from the other end of the line. He bit the inside of his cheek to keep from yelling at the damn kid. Rick's cousin was so flaky, so burned out, that he might just put the phone down and drift off.

"Come on, Wilfred," Bernie coaxed. "Where's the lawyer?"

"With Rick—in the slammer."

"Damn! Rick's in jail? How the hell'd that happen?"

"Rick was cruising the party to see if he could get the stuff on that old '47 Ford pickup, you know?"

Bernie waited. "Yeah, yeah, the truck. I know. Go on."

"Well, he got kinda nervous, so he put me out down the block to look out for him. So I was watchin', and this cop comes out of nowhere and starts searchin' Rick. I ran back behind some houses. When I looked again, Rick was in a cop car. I ran outta there. Then I looked up lawyers in the yellow pages. I called and called, finally I got one."

Bernie groaned. "Where are you now?" he asked.

"That's what I'm trying to tell you," Wilfred said. "I'm at the lawyer's office. He's gone over to spring Rick. When I called him and told him what had happened, he told me to get right over here. We talked. Then he said he'd be able to get Rick out. I never thought no one could if they busted you with that much stuff."

"So what'd you tell this lawyer?"

"I told him we brought the H up from El Paso, just like you

told us to. But he said I had to tell him everything, the way it is, if he was going to be able to get Rick off. So I, well, I had to—but he says he's worked things out real well before, even worked with the cops. And I figured, you know, I mean he says he knows practically all the guys on the state security force—he even knows you. And when I told him what was really going on, you know I figured since he was your buddy he'd maybe do more for us—so I leveled with him—"

When Bernardo spoke into the phone his voice was so low Rick's cousin could barely hear it, but so dangerous Wilfred stopped talking at once.

"Just who is this lawyer?"

"Mr. Brunalushi."

"*Aldo Brunalesci*? Does he know you're calling me?"

"No." Rick's cousin laughed uneasily. "He said not to bother you, that he'd take care of everything, that he'd let you know first thing in the morning. But, Bernie, I need some stuff. I mean, the cops took it all—"

"Listen, Wilfred," Bernie said, "don't tell Brunalesci you've talked to me, okay? I mean, it'll be our secret that I'm going to get you some stuff tonight. Okay? Just don't mention it to him. I'll just kind of drop in and surprise you, right? It'll take me about an hour to drive down to Albuquerque. You just sit tight. And remember, don't tell him you talked to me. He might not be so happy about getting Rick out if he knew that you two used the stuff."

"Okay, Bernie, but get down here soon's you can."

"Right," Bernie crooned, hanging the phone up.

"Screw it!" he yelled, kicking it across the room.

He could hear Angie stirring in the den. He yanked a heavy shirt, blue jeans, and a parka out of the closet. His hands were shaking badly. He started putting on his clothes as fast as he could and was sitting on the bed in his jeans, pulling on his boots, when Angie swiveled in the door.

"Bernie." She stared at his boots. "Bernie, where are you going?"

"Emergency. Got to go."

"But you're not in your uniform."

He ignored her, grabbing a ski sweater to pull over his shirt.

"Well," she pouted, "don't be all night."

Bernie strapped on his .38, zipped on his parka, and grabbed his wallet and keys off the dresser. He figured he had maybe an hour to get to a safe place. For a moment he worried about Angie, but, naw, she didn't know anything about it. Maybe he could call a little later and tell her to get up to her folks' place in Mora.

Right now he had to drop out of sight for awhile. He'd have to reach the governor somehow. State's evidence might save his neck, but Governor Cortés was the only one he could safely offer it to.

Without turning on the Audi's lights, he cruised out of the driveway.

FOUR

At dawn a sharp chill wind whipped through the vast flat acreage of the Estancia Valley. Cliff's old rooster crowed stridently.

In the bunkhouse, Joe woke and saw in the dimness that his uncle was already up and gone. He looked over at Rod and watched him curl more tightly around the pillow he was holding, groping in his sleep for the quilts that had slipped off the bed to the plank floor.

Joe threw off his covers, shivered in the morning air, and walked to the small window. He pulled a tobacco pouch and cigarette papers from his rumpled shirt pocket. Expertly, he rolled the cigarette with one hand and lit the end with a wooden match. He stood silently, smoking and staring through the dusty glass at the ranch house.

Cliff's rambling adobe house clung to the brown land as if anticipating the return of the relentless winds that swept across the prairie each spring, piling tumbleweeds high against its walls. Green and gray junipers spread out under the windows and at the kitchen door, where cars and pickup trucks were clustered. Piñons stood over a carpet of last year's cones and nuts. Above them, Cliff's tribladed windmill turned smoothly, generating electricity.

The rooster crowed again. Its shrill call penetrated the thick walls of the ranch house. The crowing awoke Moira and she turned over irritably. Ted stirred in his sleep and flopped a heavy arm across her chest. Moira's thin lips formed a hard line and she heaved the arm off her breasts.

In the master bedroom, Cliff and Lauren were already awake, languid from a night of lovemaking and very little sleep. At the rooster's crow, Cliff slowly rolled over and sat up on the edge of the bed. He picked up Lauren's silk slip where it lay under his feet. It smelled faintly of perfume.

"Shameless hussy." He smiled and tossed the silk at Lauren.

"Fortunate for you," she replied, her voice even huskier than usual. She opened one eye and swept the slip over the side of the bed to the floor.

"Come back here," she whispered.

Cliff went willingly, warming his naked body against her, smelling again the mysterious aroma of her skin and hair. The softness of her body made him forget the others under his roof. He slowly moved against her. Her nipples became erect.

"God," she sighed voluptuously, "this has got to be the last frontier."

The rooster had finished crowing when Cliff finally stood relaxed at the cast iron stove, scrambling eggs in a large black skillet. Behind him, at the other end of the room, Ted and Moira Findley sat silent at the big round table set with plastic mats and silverware. Two German shepherds lay on the brick floor underneath the pine table with their heads between their paws, their eyes on Cliff. Low growls started in their throats.

Cliff glanced at the back door. "It's all right," he told the dogs. "Be quiet."

Soon he himself heard the footsteps and in a few seconds the back door opened and Joe and Valencio entered. A gust of cold air arrived with them, thinning out the strong smell of bacon and coffee. Joe moved toward the table.

The dogs began to growl again and Cliff snapped his fingers loudly.

"Cinco! Seis! Be quiet!" he ordered.

When Valencio walked toward them the dogs lay down silently, noses on paws again.

"Have some coffee." Cliff jerked his head toward the table.

The Indians pulled up chairs next to Ted and Moira. She nodded at them but Ted hardly looked up. His head was propped in his hands and his eyes were red-rimmed slits in his puffy face. Joe picked up the big blue speckled enamel pot and filled two mugs. He put several spoonfuls of sugar into them and handed one to his uncle. They settled into the quiet warmth of the yellow room.

Cliff carried the eggs over to the table. He glanced at the dogs, lying quietly at Valencio's feet. Their hackles were rising again as they stared toward the door. Cliff looked out the window to see what was bothering them now. Someone was coming up the path from the bunkhouse. It was Rod— minus his flaming beard!

"Quiet!" Cliff told the dogs, He nudged one of them with the side of his boot. Valencio looked under the table at the dogs and they fell silent.

Rod shut the door quickly behind him.

"Hey, whaddya know," Cliff said, smiling broadly. "That was a good try, but I can't say it improved your looks any."

Rod went straight for the coffee pot. "Yeah, well, I made the sacrifice. It was a dead giveaway. Not many guys with red beards."

Cliff put a stack of enameled plates on the table.

"Chow down," he said. "We've got a lot to do this morning."

"Mmmm," Rod agreed, gulping his coffee. "We've got less than twenty-four hours before the hijack. Everybody's got to learn to fly. And we've got to figure out all the details.

45

"Glad you guys made it," Rod told Joe and Valencio.
They nodded.

"Valencio," Moira reproved, "why are you doing this?"

Valencio looked at her solemnly. "Many things on this earth are for sale, but Father Sun gives himself freely to all beings. Not even white eyes can sell the sun."

Cliff put a hot pan of cornbread on the table. "That's right," he said quietly. "Sunshine should be free."

Moira looked sour, Cliff thought. She had managed to get every hair in place and her cosmetic mask on, but something about her looked somehow askew.

"Okay," Rod said. "Let's begin with the tipi village. Tell me everything I need to know about it, Valencio."

The old man shrugged. "It's Hollywood's idea of a place where Indians live."

"How many tipis are there?" Rod asked. "How many people can sleep in a tipi? Can we have a fire in each one? Will they be warm enough at this time of year?"

"You shoot questions like machine gun," Valencio grunted. "The tipis are weatherproof. They were made by the Sioux for the movie company. There are six of them. One is larger."

Rod looked at Cliff. "More than enough."

"The altitude in the foothills isn't that high either," Joe added. "The temperature gets up into the forties during the day, but it's really cold at night."

"We'll need warm clothing," Rod said, "and sleeping bags. Of course, there'll be plenty of wood around and we'll have an ax."

"No fires," Valencio said shortly.

"Why not?"

"A tipi will light up like a lantern at night with a fire inside."

"What about the day? We'll be hiding in the tipis. The police will be nosing around in helicopters and small planes looking for us."

The old man shook his head. "You want to send them smoke signals?"

"Then how can we cook?"

"Coleman stove," Valencio said.

"I've got one," said Cliff. "What about water?"

"There's a creek not far away, gives enough for drinking and cooking."

"You said something last night about buildings, Valencio. A place to hide the chase cars."

"There is a place. An old barn where the movie company kept the stagecoach. It will be big enough."

"It's big enough," Joe agreed. "The other buildings are just shacks, really. There's one where we keep firewood and another full of props the movie people didn't bother to take with them when they left. The concession stand and a couple of outhouses."

"Sounds like a real posh resort," said Lauren, coming in late as usual to take the last empty chair. "I can hardly wait." She laughed good-naturedly, looking at Cliff and reaching for the remains of the scrambled eggs. "Is there anything else to eat around here? I'm starved."

"I gave my housekeeper the week off," Cliff told her. "Why don't you look around?"

Lauren scanned the contents of the refrigerator. "What about food while we're at the hideout?" she asked, holding the refrigerator door half open.

"You can help Mercedes plan that, I guess. We should be hearing from her soon."

Lauren bit into a piece of cheese and shrugged. "Might as well. I plan meals for a hundred fat ladies every day of my life."

"We'll need enough food for fourteen people," Rod said. "And I hope we're not up there longer than a day or two."

"If our protest works, public support should be quick," said Cliff.

"How can you think this insane plan is going to get public support?" Moira asked angrily. "I can't believe you all are serious." She looked around the table. "We all had too much to drink last night"—her gaze settled on her husband—"but now it's morning."

Rod leaned his chair back until it touched the wall. He ran his right hand over his bare cheek and looked directly at Moira.

"We talked this over last night, Moira," he said in a hard voice. "There comes a time when you have to make a stand for what you believe. The real issue is freedom, not taxes." He looked into each face. "If anybody wants out, say so now."

"I'm with you, captain," Cliff laughed. Lauren nodded in lazy agreement. Valencio gave a grunt. Joe nodded.

"Ted?"

"I'm in." Ted's voice was firm. He didn't look at Moira.

Spots of color burned on Moira's cheeks. "Ted," she said in polite tones, "maybe we ought to talk about it now that—"

"I said, I'm in!" he repeated, pressing his hands to his forehead.

"Well, I don't think we can just decide on the spur of the moment. I think we ought to discuss it. I mean, it's just absurd!" she finished, her voice breaking angrily.

The table was silent. Lauren continued to sip her coffee, peering over the rim of her cup at Ted, whose eyes were hidden. Everyone else looked at Moira, who tried to smile but failed.

"You'll have to decide, Moira," Rod said.

"I can't decide now. . ." Moira threw an anxious glance at Ted, then looked around the table. Everyone was still watching her. She shivered.

"All right," she said ungraciously.

Rod started to say something, but Ted spoke first. "You'd better be sure," he said in a low voice. Moira's lips trembled.

"I believe, dear," Lauren said ruthlessly, "Ted has slipped the leash."

Moira shot her a terrified look.

Ted remained silent. Rod said more gently, "It's up to you."

Moira looked at Ted. In a small voice she said, "Yes, I'll do it."

"Good for you," Lauren answered with surprising warmth.

Moira closed her eyes and pursed her lips to keep from crying.

The telephone's urgent ringing broke the awkward silence. Cliff answered, talked briefly, and hung up. "That was Mercedes," he told the others. "She has Serefina with her! They forgot the map, and they're up at Felipe's Exxon station. Serefina's not slow. She stopped her grandmother from asking directions at the gas station."

"Serefina?" asked Rod. "That's all we need, another—"

"Oh, come on, Rod," Lauren chided. "Give the girl a chance."

"Better she should be with us than against us," Cliff reminded him.

"Well, maybe. . ." Rod said dubiously. He stroked the strange smoothness of his bare face. "God, we've got so much to do!"

He stood up abruptly, knocking the back of his chair against the wall. "Everybody hurry and finish your breakfast. It's time to teach you guys to fly a balloon!"

Rod reached for his jacket from the peg by the kitchen door. "Cliff, is your balloon in the barn?"

Cliff nodded.

"Then let's go grab a pickup and get it. We can unpack it in the bean field for the balloon lesson. Valencio and Joe, you want to give us a hand?"

The group straggled out of the kitchen, zipping and buttoning their coats, and headed toward Joe's red pickup truck parked in a cluster of cottonwoods. The light snow of the day before had melted; their boots scuffed through dust and sage. Above them the blue of the sky was so intense it seemed unreal.

The Last Frontier stretched out, dotted here and there with tumbleweeds, cactus, and fine Hereford cows. The same fields Cliff planted each spring had been tilled by Pueblo Indians in prehistoric times. During the great pinto bean era, valiant homesteaders had struggled to make their living on small farms here, but recurring droughts in the twenties and thirties put an end to both homesteaders and bean farming. Now the land was sparsely populated again, given over to large cattle ranches and irrigated crops of corn, potatoes, and alfalfa.

Rod stuck his hands contentedly into the pockets of his Pendleton jacket. He inhaled deeply and gave a satisfied smile. The air smelled of piñon smoke and the promise of an early spring.

"Perfect weather for ballooning," he observed. "I hope our luck holds out and it's like this again tomorrow."

Cliff and Joe had wrestled the wicker gondola out of the pickup bed. It lay on its side on the ground, fan and battery box nearby. Valencio and Joe were rolling out the blue and white nylon.

"Come on," Cliff yelled. "Give us a hand with this thing."

They stood on opposite sides of the balloon, gently pulling at the fabric in a benign tug of war. Lauren's gloved hands slipped on the thin nylon. When they had the envelope spread out flat, she whistled. "It's as big as a tennis court," she said.

Rod stood at the narrow end. He swung his arm in an explanatory arc. "This area is called the mouth; and this part here is the skirt. Now I'll connect these cables to the basket's framework, and we'll use our fan to do the inflating."

They all watched as the huge pouch of flat material quickly gulped up the rush of cool air from the fan, seething and writhing like a dead thing burbling to life.

"Okay," Rod called over the whir of the fan. "That's enough."

The men quickly shoved the fan out of the way. Then, as Joe and Cliff held the nylon out carefully, Rod turned the burner valve and the first long hot whoosh of flame shot noisily into the belly of the balloon. Moira jumped back as she felt the heat touch her face.

"Remember," Rod shouted, "the balloon is essentially a container holding air. Warmer air makes it light so it can float. You keep the air warm and it keeps floating." Joe and Valencio went to either side of the staggering mass to hold onto it by the seams as it began to puff up into the familiar bulblike shape.

Now Rod came over to peer into the balloon. When it was inflated he walked inside, going to the far end where he seemed to be inspecting a sort of trapdoor device in the fabric.

"Wow," Lauren breathed, astounded at how dwarfed the big man was inside the giant bubble. She moved closer and stuck her head in. Sunlight filtered through the colored nylon in a curiously stained-glass effect. It was like entering a cathedral.

"What's he doing in there?" she asked Cliff over her shoulder.

"Checking the deflation system," Cliff replied. "See that rope he's bringing back? That's the ripcord. It's attached to a panel at the top of the balloon. You have the other end of the ripcord in the basket. If that deflation panel doesn't close properly after you've pulled the line, you'll drop like a shot duck."

"Oh, I wish you wouldn't say things like that, Cliff," Moira groaned, closing her eyes and moving her head from side to side.

Lauren took Moira's hand and squeezed it reassuringly. "Why are you so afraid?" she asked quietly, looking into Moira's pale face. "You and Ted have been on ground crews at the balloon meets. You've been around balloons more than most of us."

"That was Teddy's idea! I never thought I'd have to go up in one!"

Now Rod emerged from the balloon. He fastened the

ripcord to a bracket on the wicker gondola. Joe and Cliff caught hold of the long guy lines as Rod began refiring the burner. When the envelope at last rose off the ground, Rod climbed into the basket, still firing propane blasts.

"Okay, that's the easy part," he told them with a grin. He stood under what was now a beautifully round sphere. "Anyway, the balloons will already be inflated and ready to fly when we take them over tomorrow morning. It's what we do from this point on that's important. . ."

The sound of an untuned motor drowned out Rod's voice. He frowned as he saw an old yellow school bus approaching the ranch house. It swung around to the kitchen door and chugged to a stop. Mercedes and Serefina got out. Mercedes waved and disappeared inside the house. Serefina started toward the bean field.

Rod stared at the bus for a long time, then shook his head.

"Doesn't look much like a chase vehicle, does it?" Cliff said.

Rod shot Cliff a look of sudden comprehension and horror. "No way!" he snapped.

"It's perfect," Cliff said. "Who's going to suspect Our Lady of Sorrows parish bus? We couldn't have come up with something better in a million years."

Rod stared skeptically at the decrepit yellow bus. Serefina was running toward them in long, graceful strides. She wore jeans, a Navy pea jacket, and boots. Her long hair, caught back in a single braid, reflected the sun blue-black as a crow's wing.

Rod shook his head slowly.

"They can drive the bus to tipi village right after lift-off," Cliff went on persuasively. "Once we get into the mountains, we'll put a camouflage tarp over the roof. Main thing is, the bus will hold all five balloons and fit into the barn out at the tipi village."

Rod sighed. Serefina jumped lightly down the shallow embankment and came over to where they were standing.

"You're late," Rod said. "The flying lesson's already started."

The ebony eyes looked directly into his. "I'm a quick study," she said without expression.

Rod turned to the others. "Okay, first I'm going to give you general instructions and then I'll take you up in pairs. When you lift off tomorrow morning, I want it to be old stuff instead of a maiden voyage!

"Taking off and landing are the dangerous phases of ballooning, as they are in all flying," Rod said. "Now, your main tool during lift-off is this blast valve. Without it, you can't climb and you can't stay up."

Moira gave a nervous laugh.

Rod glanced at her appraisingly and continued. "Think of the blast valve as the gas pedal in your car. When you turn the valve, it's like stepping on the gas—but instead of speed, you get height. Okay, after you blast, give the heat time to circulate. Then, if the balloon doesn't rise as high or as fast as you want, give it another blast." He looked at the group. "Everybody understand?"

They all nodded, though the effort made Ted grimace.

"Okay, then come over here close to the basket." The group moved as one toward him. "See these three tanks in the corners?" He pointed. "They hold more propane than we need to get us from the balloon field to tipi village.

"See these three dials? That's the only instrument panel you have. This is the altimeter, it tells you how high you are—" Rod hesitated, watching Moira's lips move as she stared with intense concentration at the three dials. "Don't worry about these details right now," he said to her in a soft voice. "It'll make a lot more sense when you're up in the air."

He straightened and addressed the whole group.

"Now, about landing. The ripcord opens the deflation panel at the top and lets the hot air out. When you pull the ripcord, you cool the balloon and lose altitude."

He looked at the women, each in turn. Lauren looked interested. Serefina met his eyes impassively. Moira's head was bent, her gloved hand over her eyes.

"It takes a lot of strength to yank the deflation panel open.

You women may have to get your passenger to help you pull the ripcord. Pull the rope together. But use your ripcord carefully or you'll—"

"Drop like a shot duck," finished Lauren. Moira made a mewing sound.

"Well, who's first? I'll take two of you."

Serefina stepped forward and climbed agilely into the gondola. Rod shifted uncomfortably once she was beside him. She smiled a little, her teeth white in her wind-burned face.

Ted suddenly stepped up to the gondola. "I'll go, too."

Moira reached out a hand, then dropped it.

"Put the hard hats on," Cliff directed. "They're down there under the instrument panel."

"Why do we have to wear those?" Lauren eyed them disdainfully.

"In case the burner falls on your head when you're landing," Rod explained.

"Oh," Lauren said. She smiled at him and shrugged.

Suddenly the burner roared and the balloon lifted off the ground and climbed steadily upward. Cliff put his arm around Moira's shoulders. "Well, we're the chase crew, let's get in the truck."

"What about us?" Joe asked, but Valencio was climbing stoically into the pickup bed.

Serefina was astonished at how the ground seemed to fall gently away. There was no jolt or even especially any feeling of ascent. It was just that Cliff, Lauren, Moira, and the two Indian men grew smaller. Then she was looking down on the field, the house and windmill, and the tiny red truck.

The sky was clear, the sun was bright, and it was warmer in the balloon than on the ground. Rod seemed to catch her thought. "We're going with the wind, offering no resistance, so the chill factor has dropped. That's why it doesn't seem as cold up here."

Serefina noticed he avoided looking at her as he spoke. She

stared at him mischievously. This tall, broad-shouldered man seemed uneasy with her. She liked him better than she had at the Findleys'. He was competent with the balloon. And now that the wild red beard was gone, she saw he had a strong jaw.

"We're ascending at two hundred feet per minute. I'll go up a few thousand feet and then let you both take us up and down until you get the feel of it. We'll also try to catch some currents for direction."

Suddenly Ted burped loudly. "You okay?" Rod asked. Ted shook his head; his face was pale. The two men stared at each other unhappily. Ted retched.

"Lean over this side, for heaven's sake!" Serefina commanded. "Away from the wind!"

Ted hung over the side of the gondola. Rod looked at Serefina, and under his steady gaze she smiled.

"What made you come?" he asked abruptly.

"I didn't understand what this was all about last night," she said. "It sounded preposterous, hijacking hot-air balloons to talk to the archbishop and the governor. It took quite a while for my grandmother to make it clear."

"And now that she has?" Rod asked gruffly.

"I am one of you." Serefina raised her fist in mock seriousness.

Rod's smile, she noticed, began slowly and gradually lit up his whole face. She liked that especially. She decided he deserved a better explanation.

"What especially made me decide to throw my eggs in this basket"—she patted the wicker and smiled at her own pun—"is that I don't believe this tax is random stupidity."

Rod looked at her intently.

She said, "We archeologists work with the state monuments department, and we're losing a battle with the uranium companies over Pueblo Cebollita."

"The Anasazi Indian ruins near Chaco Canyon?"

"Yes, you know Chaco Canyon?"

"I've been reading about some work done up there," Rod

said. "They've measured the temperatures on the terraces of the Pueblo Cebollita ruins, which are about sixty-five degrees on a twenty-degree winter day. The place is an eighteen-hundred-year-old giant solar collector."

"Really! Then you'll know what I'm talking about when I say I think the people who built the ancient pueblos were pretty sophisticated."

Rod nodded agreement.

"So do you know about the outriders?"

"No, what are they?"

"Ceremonial fire spots on eight-mile radii from the pueblo. And guess what's under each one?"

"Not . . . uranium ore?"

Serefina nodded. "At least, so they say. And the uranium companies that mine in that part of the state have really brought pressure to be allowed to mine it. Of course, that will ruin the outriders."

They drifted silently for a moment. Then Serefina went on. "What's most terrible to me is that the amount of ore underneath the outriders is relatively small. It's as if there's a determination to destroy."

"You think you can stop the uranium companies by stopping the sunshine tax?"

"Yes, because I think most people would choose solar power if they understood how it works."

"Yeah," Rod said quietly. "I know what you mean."

They looked at each other warmly and then quickly turned away, Rod with studious attention to the altimeter and pyrometer, Serefina to inquire how Ted felt.

"Better now," he told her.

"Okay," Rod said. "Then let's finish the lesson."

In the kitchen of the ranch house, Mercedes was roasting green chiles. She laid them on top of the cookstove until the skins browned and popped, flipping them with a fork until they were scorched on all sides. Then she wrapped them in a damp dishtowel and sat down at the table to peel off the crisp skins so she could make a pot of posole.

As she peeled the chiles she reviewed the altar society members. Serefina would drive the bus, of course. Mrs. Casaus and Maria Atencio would without question agree to do the needles . . . for the church. That meant two more people were needed. Mercedes thought Mrs. Casaus's daughter-in-law could be persuaded. No one else was trustworthy unless she asked Concha, but Concha was so slow, such a *boba*. Donaldo Anaya's mother would be willing, but she was eighty-two and might not have the strength. It would be better to use her to deliver the ransom note. Maybe Concha was the only other possibility. Well, no need to worry about it now, this afternoon was soon enough.

Mercedes dumped the peeled chiles into the boiling pot and threw the scorched skins away. She licked her finger absently. Aiee, Chihuahua . . . this posole would clear their sinuses!

Cliff and Rod followed the others to the ranch house after putting away the balloon.

"Whadda you think, can they do it?" Cliff asked.

"They can all fly a balloon, if that's what you mean," Rod said. "But I don't know about Moira Findley. Is she going to hang in or freak out?"

"And if she freaks out?"

"For openers, she could give away the location of the hideout and blow the whole thing."

"You're right. We've gotta find out now what she'll do when the chips are down. We can't afford to wait until tomorrow morning."

"How can we force the issue?"

Cliff squinted toward the house where the others were going in the back door. "Tonight, when we assign the balloons, tell her she's going to be taking up one by herself. That'll be enough pressure to see if she cracks."

"What will we do if she falls apart?"

Cliff scuffed along a few steps, picked up a rock, and threw it at a clump of sagebrush. "Put her in Lauren's custody," he said. "A week at the Enchanted Door wouldn't hurt her at all."

Rod laughed and put his hand on Cliff's shoulder. "Thanks, Leftenant Randall. Now that we've completed our cracked squadron with Flying Ace Findley, let's inspect our transportation."

The old school bus stood high off the ground, its faded side lettered: OUR LADY OF SORROWS PARISH. An inspection showed that the back of the bus had been completely removed and replaced by two wooden doors. Rod pulled on one tentatively. Both doors opened outward, and a contraption that had been folded up on the inside opened down at the same time, making three sturdy steps.

There were only two rows of seats on the bus, the driver's and the row behind it. The rest of the bus was empty. It was like a high-ceilinged vacant garage on wheels.

"Yeaaaahhh," Cliff murmured approvingly as he peered inside. "We can carry lots of stuff in here."

Rod looked doubtful. "Coming back there'll be over a dozen people and five packed gondolas," he reminded his friend.

"So we sit in the baskets," Cliff suggested.

They heard a step behind them. Serefina stood there, wiping her hands on a large white apron.

"How do you like it?" she asked. "The doors were Father Paul's idea. Now it is easier for him to bring communion to the tiny villages. We removed the big table, of course, knowing you needed room for the balloons."

Rod kicked at one of the tires. "What kind of shape is this thing in mechanically?"

"Well, the parish has had it for a very long time," Serefina said slowly. "And it was old before they got it, I understand. But there's probably nothing on it I couldn't fix."

Rod crawled under the bus without further comment and lay on his back looking up at its innards.

Cliff smiled at Serefina. "Then you're a mechanic, too?" he asked.

"I learned what I thought I should know to take a jeep into the badlands by myself. There are no garages or service stations there."

Rod wiggled out from under the bus and stood up, brushing dust and sand off the seat of his pants. He raked his fingers through his wiry red hair, shaking his head.

He went around to the front of the bus and after a great deal of tugging and yanking, succeeded in getting the rusty yellow hood open. Serefina and Cliff followed and stood silently as he peered inside, muttering incoherently all the while. When he withdrew his head, he turned on Serefina.

"Why don't they take care of this thing?" he asked. "It hasn't been greased in years, the muffler's ready to fall off, the oil's filthy, the fan belt's rotten—"

"Listen," she said, "I am not the parish grease monkey. Until today I had never before been in this bus. I drive the anthropology department's jeep and take care of it myself when I do—with no complaints from the university. Anything you can't handle, I probably can." Her eyes flashed warningly.

Cliff said quickly, "Okay, get it greased, change the oil this afternoon, and I'm sure we'll make it."

"No doubt!" Serefina said coldly. Then she turned on her heel abruptly and walked toward the house, the long braid down her back twitching angrily.

"Now what the hell did I say?" Rod asked Cliff.

"If you don't know now, Riley, I can't explain."

Rod banged the hood of the bus shut.

"Rod," Cliff said, "relax. If this isn't going to be fun, what's the point of doing it?"

Rod turned and said bitterly, "Funny, Cliff, very hilarious!"

Lauren came up to them. "Supper is ready." Then she

asked Rod, "What'd you do to Serefina? She came in like a dust devil, talking a thousand miles a minute in Spanish, and it all sounded obscene."

Cliff jerked his head toward Rod. "They're in love," he said.

Lauren studied Rod's scowl for a minute, then whistled.

"But for me," Cliff said, "good old-fashioned lust. It's so much less complicated!" He pulled Lauren to him and kissed her.

A late model dark-green Plymouth sedan passed through the gates of the National Cemetery in Santa Fe just before sunset and moved slowly around the loop. When it reached Section III, it came to a stop where some bare lilac bushes grew close to the curb. State Security Chief Hans Daggett, a big man in his fifties with a bulldog face, rolled his window down a crack and looked around. It was very quiet. The rows of identical white tombstones cast long shadows on the faded winter lawns, the plastic flower wreaths, and empty green vases. The place was deserted.

Daggett looked at his wristwatch, then turned up the collar of his topcoat. He peeled the cellophane off a cigar and plugged in the cigarette lighter. He flipped on the radio.

. . .balloon festival will cost Albuquerque two hundred thousand dollars this year. The Chamber of Commerce notes that some of that amount was supplied by the city, raised through a lodgers' tax collected from motels . . .

With one move of his huge hand, Daggett shut off the radio and pulled out the lighter, touching it to the cigar. Soon ribbons of smoke began drifting out the car window toward the leafless lilac bushes.

He smoked impatiently for several minutes before the car he was looking for appeared in the rearview mirror. He watched as it pulled up behind him. The man who got out

60

wore a brown corduroy jacket. He was short and bald. He glanced around casually as he approached the Plymouth. "Chief," he greeted Daggett.

"What's so important, Tige?" Chief Daggett asked around his cigar.

"Brunalesci sent me up here because the governor has an informant who can blow apart the heroin operation in this state."

"It's been tried before. No one knows enough to do us any damage."

"This time the informant can put us away," Tige said, watching him carefully. "Brunalesci said to tell you it's your lieutenant, Bernie Martinez."

"Bernie? The hell you say! Where'd you get a crazy idea like that? Bernie's worked with us for the past fifteen years!"

"Consider yourself lucky that Brunalesci found out like he did. Otherwise, we mighta wondered how come your right-hand man was moonlighting."

"What happened?" Daggett growled.

"Some punk got picked up with five keys of quality H last night. Five keys, top grade! By dumb luck, his cousin called Brunalesci to defend him. Brunalesci knew right away it was syndicate heroin. No street punk's gonna get ahold of that much good stuff, so he pumped them. Their story is that Bernie Martinez gives them the heroin to plant on an old truck that belongs to some kinda hippie named Rodriguez Riley who travels up north fairly regular."

Daggett's face fell into ferocious folds. "Riley? How's he figure in?"

"I get the idea he's not involved. The kids say the stuff was planted on his truck. They always had instructions from Bernie to keep it a secret from Riley."

"Well, hell, Riley has to know."

Tige rubbed his fingers back and forth over his shiny head. "But the kids claim—"

"Would you tell two dumb punks like that your courier

knew what was happening?" Daggett asked. "Nah, Bernie kept them in the dark. That bastard Bernie would be in the clear now if they hadn't called Brunalesci. Lucky coincidence for us."

Tige said, "Brunalesci thinks you better get rid of Bernie. You've got to find him, get to him fast before the governor gets back from Texas. New York will have all our asses on a shingle if this gets out of hand. Brunalesci told them you could handle things."

"I'll get on it. Meanwhile, where's Riley?"

Tige shrugged uncomfortably. "Well, his truck's still outside the house on Rio Grande where the kids were picked up last night."

"Yeah?"

"But nobody's home—"

Daggett interrupted impatiently. "Keep someone on that truck. Watch it every minute. We got to pick Riley up and find out what he knows. Then we'll dump him and his truck off a mountain road somewhere. I'll get that frigging Bernie if it's the last thing I do. You find Riley wherever he is!"

Tige nodded abruptly and left the car. Daggett sat there for a long time after Tige had left. Finally, he flipped his cigar butt onto the cemetery lawn, rolled up the car window, cleaned the steam off the inside of the windshield with an angry swipe of his hand, and drove off as slowly and silently as he had come.

Joe and Valencio sat motionless on the edge of the dry arroyo below Cliff's ranch house.

"This hijack," Joe said finally, " . . . a big risk."

Valencio stared fixedly at the lowering sun.

"And will anyone listen?" Joe asked.

"Mebbe," his uncle grunted. "Mebbe not."

Joe watched the old man out of the side of his eyes for a long time. Valencio smoked silently, raising the cigarette to his creased brown lips with an almost ceremonial gesture. Joe hunkered down and watched the small birds that were beginning to flutter through the bare branches. Valencio continued looking at the sun.

For a few brief moments red and gold flowed over the landscape, changing the yellow school bus to orange and the earth tones of the ranch buildings to glowing rose. The sun's last rays touched the windows of the house, turning them into gold mirrors. Gradually, the colors began to fade. Then the subtle pastel hues of the desert dulled to gray and tan, and the sun disappeared below the distant horizon.

Valencio rose and Joe followed him back to the ranch house.

Firelight flickered softly in the living room at the Last Frontier. Joe and Valencio were seated cross-legged close to the warmth. Rod sank into a wing chair. Lauren sprawled on her belly on a handsome Navajo rug before the fireplace. Ted and Moira were across the room at either end of the leather couch, and Cliff walked around topping everyone's coffee from a bottle of Myers.

"Don't go to sleep, woman," he said as he added rum to Lauren's cup. "We've still got work to do." She stared dreamily into the fire.

Rod took a noisy slurp of his coffee, then raised himself out of the chair with a groan. "Yes, we have a couple of things to wrap up before we hit the sack. We have to be up again in"—he checked his watch—"five hours."

"Five hours!" Lauren moaned.

Ted asked, "Then we'll be getting up at three A.M.? So we ought to get to Cutter Field about six in the morning?"

"That's right," Rod confirmed. "Before she took off, Serefina said she'd drive the bus over about that time, maybe a little later, try to come in with the first crowds."

"We're not going to go home first?" Moira asked irritably. "I thought Rod was going to pick up his truck at our house before . . . " she trailed off bitterly.

"We don't need my truck," Rod answered, "since we can use the parish bus for a chase car."

Moira sighed wearily. She ran her hand along the arm of the couch; the feel of the good leather comforted her. She had been surprised at the interior of Cliff's house. Several excellent old Acoma pots sat in the deep shelves on either side of the fireplace, their fine geometric designs dramatic against the whitewashed wall. The living room was strangely narrow, yet the heavy furniture was gracefully placed and the general effect was both comfortable and elegant.

Rod had moved over to the rolltop desk at the far end of the room and was shuffling through some papers. "Here," he said, "I've cut pictures of your target balloons out of the festival program. They're in color, with the names under them. Underneath each picture I've written the number of the balloon's launching site and the CB handle you'll answer to."

Lauren said, "Let's get it over with fast. I still have to drive back to the Enchanted Door to get the champagne."

Cliff put his hand on the back of her neck and rubbed it slightly. "We can make it in the morning. We'll have time before the mass ascension. If we get back to Albuquerque by six, you'll have time to pack the brunches."

"I guess so," Lauren yawned.

Rod reached into his back pants pocket and pulled out a folded newspaper clipping. "I've got the map of the balloon field here with this year's proposed layout, although there may be some last-minute changes. *Sun Power* is in location A7. . ."

He handed a picture to Cliff, who consulted the newspaper diagram. "J3," Cliff read, "*Rainbow's End*."

Rod picked up another picture. "Ted, how would you like to take up our lovely lieutenant governor? The lady who actually signed the sunshine tax into law?"

Ted came over quickly to take the picture from Rod's hand. He looked at the name under the photograph of a green-and-gray striped balloon, *Windfoal*. Rod had written under it, "R16." He showed Ted how the field was laid out with the letters along the long edge and the numbers along the short side.

"Here, Joe," Rod said, "you and Valencio can take up the archbishop." Joe leaned over to look at the photograph of the *Artful Dodger*, a bright orange balloon with a chevron design.

"Moira?" Rod looked past the others to where she sat alone and silent on the big sofa. "Here's what your balloon looks like."

"*My* balloon? I thought I was going up with Ted."

"No, you're not." Rod said. "We need you to fly the commissioner." He held out his hand, offering her the small square picture of the *Camelot*, a pure white balloon with a large red British cross of St. George.

Moira looked over at Ted but he avoided her eyes. She stared at the rest of them, swallowing. They all looked calmly back at her. She hesitated for what seemed like a long time before slowly walking over to accept the picture.

Valencio put another log on the fire and the sweet scent of cedar filled the room. "Okay," Rod said, "we have to get the balloons up, away, and down in less than an hour tomorrow morning." He walked over to the fireplace and spread a map on the hearth.

"Here's Cutter Field, our takeoff point," he said as he squatted to touch the map. "And here"—he moved his finger northeast—"is roughly where you'll land, about five minutes from the tipi village."

"Why don't we land right at the village?" Lauren asked.

"It's in the forest," Joe explained. "A small clearing. We need more room to land."

Lauren said something else, but yawned so that her words were unintelligible.

Cliff said, "When you land tomorrow, get right out of your balloon and start packing it up. Serefina and Mercedes should be there in the bus. Remember, your passenger should think we're all landing to have a champagne brunch, so I don't expect trouble from any of them."

"Yeah," Rod agreed, "keep it light. Just get the balloons packed quickly. Tell them the bus will take us to the picnic site."

"Will they believe us?" Moira asked.

"Why not?" Valencio said.

Moira dropped her eyes. She was really going to have to go through with it.

"Serefina will pick you up in the bus," Rod continued. "It should be too early to have to worry about search planes, but just in case, we'll have a tarp for the bus. Joe and Valencio will sweep the snow with branches to wipe out landing marks and tire tracks.

"That about takes care of it," Rod said, "and, remember, no real names over the air!"

"That's important," Cliff added. "We'll be using the walkie-talkies I use during roundup. They don't have great range, but they'll do to get us airborne. After that, we'll have a portable radio to keep in touch with the news."

"Did I miss anything?" Rod asked. "What do you think?"

"That this is exactly," Lauren yawned, "the kind of half-assed operation that somehow always manages to succeed by the seat of its pants!"

FIVE

Dawn. And fog, which was unusual for the high desert. Rod squinted up at the mountain, a dark hulk against the saffron glow. From behind its eleven-thousand-foot crest, weak rays of winter sunlight were just beginning to pierce the early morning haze. The hijack was about to begin.

At the edge of the launch site, Rod raised his binoculars. Trying to appear no more than a casual spectator, he searched for the other raiders in the semidarkness of the balloon field. The fog made it hard to identify figures in the sparse crowd.

Pickups were arriving one after another now. Sleepy crews unpacked and unrolled the bright nylon envelopes that would fill with hot air, growing gloriously fat and buoyant. Rod jumped at the sudden roar of a propane burner near him. Balloons writhed and began to lurch upright all around.

Rod spotted Ted and Moira. Lauren and Cliff had dropped them off at six o'clock and gone to the Enchanted Door to fix the brunches. He swept the field with the binoculars, locating Lauren by the broadcasting booth. That meant Cliff was back. Yeah, there he was, leaning against his Scout, smoking a cigarette. But where were Joe and Valencio? And where in hell was the parish bus!

"Come on, come on!" Rod muttered. He shook his head in

disgust. A goddam altar society! Too many possible mess-ups, too many people. Cliff and I should have done this alone, he thought, just the two of us like the old days.

The sun was beginning to evaporate the mist. Rod downed the last grainy bit of coffee from the hot foam cup, crushed it in his fist, and put the pieces in his pocket. His face felt cold without its woolly red blanket. He hadn't been without a beard for nine years, but without the beard he had at least a fifty-fifty chance of not being spotted by Kate. The knitted cap he wore kept springing back stiffly from his wiry hair, and he yanked it down over his ears again.

The PA system began to blurt the high-frequency squeals that always preceded opening announcements.

"Good morning, everyone," a voice began cheerfully. "Welcome to Albuquerque, balloon capital of the world and home of the *Double Eagle II* and its three courageous pilots, first balloonists to conquer the Atlantic."

That meant lift-offs would start in a few minutes. Rod checked his watch. He reached for his walkie-talkie to make a final check, hoping to raise the altar-society bus this time.

Using the code names they'd memorized last night, he called the roster.

"Stinger, Stinger, Solar Bear calling the Stinger!"

No answer from Mercedes or the altar society.

"Marlboro?"

"Ten-four," Cliff's easy voice replied.

"Ready?"

"You bet!"

"Gilda?"

"Ready," Lauren's mellow reply came a moment later.

"Lady?"

"Ready," Moira said tightly.

"Professor?"

"Ready." Ted sounded cold.

"Geronimo?"

"Here," Joe answered.

"About time! Crazy Fox with you?"

"He'll be along."

"He'd better be!" Rod growled. Then he tried again. "Stinger?"

Silence.

"Stinger, Stinger, this is Solar Bear. Come in, please!"

Still nothing.

He called to Lauren to double-check. "Your stuff all set?" he asked.

"No problem," she answered in her husky voice. That meant the decoy breakfasts would be ready when it was time to get rid of the five ground crews. Okay, great. But where in hell was the altar society and the parish bus?

Mercedes knows the whole raid depends on her needles, for Chrissakes, Rod thought. How could we have bought the idea of using little old ladies as the strike force? We should have found some other way to get rid of the pilots. But Cliff had thought it was funny.

"The señoras in that old bus are perfect," he had insisted. Well, Cliffo, Rod brooded, they're late! And without them, we can forget the whole thing.

The pale sun had driven most of the fog away now and the sky was a clear winter blue. The PA system crackled and came to life again.

"Ladies and gentlemen," said the voice from the briefing tower. "It is my pleasure today to present five of our most distinguished state officials, who not only support the balloon festival each year but will participate today as passengers in our opening event, the mass ascension. Governor Juan Cortés, Lieutenant Governor Betty Morrison, U.S. Senator George Claridge, Albuquerque City Commissioner Allan Blake, and His Excellency Archbishop Roland Grignard. Thank you very much."

Damn, they were going to start right on time! Rod grabbed the binoculars again, knocking his nose as he zeroed in on the highway. Suddenly the glasses stopped their sweep as if they had slammed into an invisible wall. They focused on a decrepit school bus mired in the bumper-to-bumper traffic approaching Cutter Field from about half a mile away. Most of the drivers in the long line had their heads out the car windows and were gawking at the balloons. Rod groaned in desperation.

He started running toward the yellow bus. *They had to have those needles!*

As he ran off the edge of the field, realizing what a distance he had yet to cover to reach the bus, the ancient yellow vehicle made a violent right-angle turn off the highway. It lurched dangerously over a deep rut parallel to the road and started bouncing across the mesa in his direction. Slowly it rocked through clumps of rabbit bush and chamisa.

Rod stopped in his tracks. Festival officials directing traffic on the highway were waving their arms and shouting. One of them leaped into a jeep and headed after the bus at top speed. The bus kept on doggedly, closing up to the very edge of the launching site where it ground to a sharp halt, its front wheels in a foot of sand. The black lettering on its venerable yellow side faced the jeep: OUR LADY OF SORROWS PARISH.

The jeep slowed. As its driver hesitated, the door of the bus opened and five elderly Spanish ladies climbed out slowly, one by one. A short black-clad figure Rod recognized as Mercedes assisted the others down the high steps.

Rod watched the pursuing jeep stop, start, stop again, and then double back toward the freeway, its driver honking and motioning frantically out the window at the handful of vehicles that had dared to follow the altar society's lead.

A slim figure stood in the open doorway of the yellow bus. It was Serefina. Her ivory oval face stood out against the dark collar of her coat. Dark-fringed eyes calmly observed the situation. She seemed satisfied that the bus would not be questioned now and turned back into it. Her black hair fell to her waist, tied back with thick white yarn. The bus door closed, and she drove skillfully off the rim of the field and headed back to the road.

Rod turned away, walking quickly through the dirt and

scruffy dried grasses. Before him, the whole field was a maze of balloons—hundreds of them, scattered about like bright toys abandoned by some giant child. Striped balloons, checkered balloons, apple and grapefruit balloons, balloons with animal pictures on them, balloons with diamond designs, a Budweiser balloon, a world globe balloon. They rippled and swayed above their baskets, not quite fat enough yet to sail the skies. The air was filled with the roar of burners.

Rod tried to locate each of the target balloons. *Camelot's* white fabric stood out among all the colors; not far from it he saw the green and gray of the *Windfoal*. Farther down the field he found the *Rainbow's End*, still somewhat limp. *Artful Dodger* was up near the parking area. His own silver sphere, the *Sun Power*, was closest to him, and he angled off a bit to avoid passing too near his ex-wife and the crew.

He pulled his cap down again to hide the telltale red hair and took outsized mirrored glasses from a pocket of the shapeless old coat a departing ranch hand had left in Cliff's bunkhouse.

The public address system squawked:

"Ladies and gentlemen. The mass ascension will begin shortly. This year, hundreds of hot-air balloons will be in the air at once. For safety purposes, we remind the pilots to wait until they receive official permission before lifting off. Ten launch directors are on the field in blue-and-white striped jackets. They will give the thumbs-up signal to each balloon individually. Please wait your turn."

An excited murmur rose from the spectators. Rod blew on his hands to warm them, conscious of the growing size of the crowd. Several thousand people were milling around on the field now. They pushed past him to get as close as possible to the balloons, laughing in short bursts of steamy breath, bumping into one another, sloshing coffee and hot chocolate out of the styrofoam cups they carried from the concession stands.

Rod noticed a short bald man in a tight-fitting brown

corduroy jacket standing alone near the *Sun Power*. He was eating a green chile burrito from a paper plate and watching Kate as she positioned and fired her burner. The man seemed to be looking for someone special in the group around the solar balloon, for his eyes darted from face to face. Then the bald man dropped the plate of half-eaten burrito onto the dirt and moved off into the flow of people.

Moira tucked manicured fingers into the elastic waistband of her down ski jacket, easing the puckered fabric around her midriff. She had stationed herself near the *Camelot*, her target balloon, and was observing its red-capped crew at work. The balloon was almost upright and they were holding the short ropes out from the rim while the pilot fired the torch.

Suddenly she heard a burst of static from the field broadcasting system:

". . . to the booth at the east end of the field. Repeat," the voice said. "The Enchanted Door Beauty Ranch has donated champagne breakfasts for crews carrying the governor and other dignitaries. Crews of *Windfoal, Camelot, Rainbow's End, Artful Dodger,* and *Sun Power*, come on in and get your champagne!" The voice cut out.

Moira heard a whoop from one of *Camelot's* crew. As she watched, spectators were taking over the ropes for them; the crew's red caps began bobbing toward the booth. Lauren had been absolutely right—they couldn't refuse free champagne!

Moira looked around her now with growing concern. Someone from the altar society was supposed to be here by this time! She started to tremble.

She moved closer to the *Camelot*; its white nylon fabric was stretched almost taut. The huge balloon lurched with a blast of the burner and Moira jumped back. She looked at the pilot standing beside the small wicker basket. Oh, I hope I can go through with this, she whispered to herself.

She tried to calm down by looking at the people around her. How much larger the crowd was this year than last! There were all types, old and young. Couples with babies snatched from damp cribs, young singles checking each other out from sheer habit, snowcapped retirees not usually out of their beds at this hour.

Moira began to circle the huge balloon as she had been instructed. With a small shock, she recognized one of the men holding onto the basket in the absence of the crew. It was Rod, wearing funny mirror glasses and a cap pulled down to his eyebrows! Near him, Moira suddenly saw the altar-society lady. She was moving up to the pilot, her dark shawl against his white flight suit, smiling pleasantly, and yes, she was asking him questions about the balloon. The young man was slim and handsome, a self-assured type whose friends would undoubtedly give him a bad time about this later. He flashed a smile at the little lady who might have been a friend of his mother's. He was answering her with patience and respect, leaning in over the edge of the *Camelot*'s wicker gondola and pointing up at the burner mounted on the bamboo overhead. The woman leaned over the gondola, too, shorter than he and close against him now. But she was not really looking up, Moira could see. Moira saw her make a quick jabbing motion and then as quickly slip something into her pocket.

Oh, God, that was her cue!

"Good morning, Commissioner Blake!" Moira called out pleasantly, as if she were playing hostess at home. She extended her hand graciously and he turned to take it, a tentative smile on his face as he frantically searched the file for her name.

"Isn't this a beautiful morning for a balloon ride?" she began, hearing her own voice as if from far away. But in that instant, the commissioner realized the pilot had slumped to the ground and was lying there absolutely still. A little old lady in black bent over him, shaking him by the shoulder.

"Señor! Señor! Are you all right?"

There was no response. Moira and the commissioner peered down into the young man's face, suddenly so pale. The somberly dressed old woman looked into Moira's eyes and nodded imperceptibly before disappearing into the crowd.

Spectators swarmed around the fallen pilot. Someone placed a rolled-up sweater under his head, and a man was rubbing his hands briskly. A third person had put a flask to his lips and was trying to get him to drink from it.

Rod pushed through the group and knelt beside the pilot. He shook him vigorously, asking, "You all right, old buddy? You all right?" He raised the unconscious pilot to his feet and managed to get one of the limp arms around his neck, where he held it securely. "Let me through, please," he demanded, half carrying, half dragging his burden in the direction of First Aid Headquarters. "I'll take care of my friend."

They must have covered thirty yards before Rod cut off to the edge of the field where campers and trailers were parked. He had to find someplace to conceal the unconscious man. He moved in between a VW bus and a metallic blue van painted with a moonlit beach scene. Its door wasn't quite closed. What luck! He took a quick look around. No one was watching. The van door slid open smoothly and silently. With one swift motion, he dumped the pilot inside on the azure shag carpet and closed the door.

Moira stood as if frozen.

"*Get him in!*" a voice grated in her ear. She looked at the speaker blankly, seeing her own terrified reflection in the mirror lenses.

"*Get him aboard!*" Rod ordered through clenched teeth.

Moira stepped forward. "Let's get into the balloon, Commissioner Blake."

"But . . ." Blake began. "What about the pilot?"

"There you go!" Moira urged him over the side of the basket and climbed in after him. The astonished commissioner stared at her.

She reached up with icy fingers and grasped the burner valve. It responded with a huge flame and a great roar. At first the *Camelot* didn't react, but then she felt the floor moving beneath her feet.

"Hands off!" she cried. She saw the startled look on Rod's face as he and the others holding the restraining ropes let go. She shot the burner again. The basket angled off. It skidded and dragged, leaving a trail of dust. It almost knocked down a trio of senior citizens who skittered out of the way. Then suddenly the *Camelot* was airborne.

"What? Oh, my!" Blake blubbered.

Moira realized at once they were headed for the power lines bordering the field.

"My God," she gasped, closing her hand on cold metal. She managed to turn the valve again. The power lines swung away beneath them.

"That white balloon took off without permission!" the voice from the briefing tower shouted excitedly. "Pilots *must* wait for permission to lift off! Repeat, *you must wait for the launch director's okay!*"

Moira looked at Blake. He was staring down at the electric wires. His pudgy fingers clung to the railing and he seemed somehow to have diminished in size.

"Your first balloon ride?" she asked.

"First and last." His voice quavered. His face was gray and his eyes blinked rapidly. Why, he's more scared than I am, Moira realized, and felt some of her own fear vanish.

She reached down for the thermos of brandy. "Here," she told him. "Drink this and you'll feel better."

Like a small obedient child whose mother has told him to finish his milk, he drained the cup without a word and reached for the thermos again.

Moira took several deep breaths and felt her body relaxing. The big balloon was moving very smoothly now. She looked down. The balloon field was now somewhat to the south. Several other balloons had lifted off.

Concha inched toward the *Windfoal*. "Green and gray balloon, green and gray balloon," she kept repeating to herself. She felt in the deep pocket of her dark skirt for the hypodermic. She spotted her target. Her thumb touched the plunger. She jabbed.

"*Idiota!* That was not the pilot!" came Mercedes's fierce whisper behind her as the man sank to the ground.

"But he has a green and gray uniform—"

"That's a gas station uniform, Concha," Mercedes said in exasperation. "Never mind, I'll take care of this myself."

Mercedes moved in swiftly. All eyes were on the prostrate mechanic from Joe Bob's Service Station. The pilot bent over him. Mercedes's needle found its mark.

Lt. Gov. Betty Morrison stood in the *Windfoal* with her sturdy legs planted apart, ready for any eventuality. The scarf at her neck exactly matched the shade of her lipstick and brought out a becoming flush in her cheeks. She was smiling.

"Fantastic!" she exclaimed. "This is just fantastic!"

Ted was concerned only with the balloon. *Windfoal* seemed easily maneuverable and they were rising smoothly, slanting up in the blue air. His passenger leaned dangerously over the side, watching the reddish dirt rectangle of the balloon field grow smaller and smaller below. The day was chilly but bright.

"Don't lean out so far," Ted told the lieutenant governor sharply.

"I hadn't realized I was doing it," she said, turning toward him with an apologetic laugh. "It's just so smooth up here! Not too different from an airplane, really."

"No, it isn't," he agreed.

Miss Morrison settled herself securely against the railing of the gondola and put her hands into her pockets. She began counting the balloons in the air.

It was Ted's first opportunity to actually get a good look at the lieutenant governor. She was younger than Moira, but not by much, he thought. Maybe a little shorter and ten pounds heavier. Her breasts were larger—an entirely different build. The short curly hair was dark blonde, and its occasional bleached streaks looked as if they were from a swimming pool rather than a beauty parlor.

"I wonder what could have caused those two guys to pass out like that?" she asked.

Ted didn't answer. He was experimenting cautiously with the controls in hopes of catching the air current Rod had promised would be up there.

Suddenly he realized they were overtaking the *Camelot*, which just moments before had seemed so far above them. He gave the burner a couple of short turns. Then the *Windfoal* was right alongside his wife's balloon, the two balloons almost bumping.

"Are you okay, Te—professor?" Moira called.

"Of course, I'm okay!" His voice bristled. Ted saw that Allan Blake had a cup in one hand and a thermos in the other.

"The commissioner's not too happy," Moira told Ted with a meaningful look. "It seems he's afraid of heights. I've given him some brandy to calm him down."

Blake looked over at them with a lopsided grin on his face.

"Well, well," he said, raising his cup as if making a toast, "if it isn't Brass Balls Betty!"

An instant change came over Betty Morrison. Her face, which had been so open and friendly, turned livid, and she gave the commissioner a deadly stare.

In an attempt to remedy the situation, Ted blasted the burner. The *Windfoal* rose easily.

"I never did like that man," the lieutenant governor told Ted in a steely voice, her lips hardly moving. "The only reason he was elected was that there were so many candidates that year the vote was splintered. There is no way a person of his mentality will ever attain a position of real power." Then she gave a short laugh. "That's off the record, okay?"

In silence the *Windfoal* floated along, now among a crowd of bright balloons. Looking at the other balloons, Ted felt that his own was sinking somewhat. It was like being in a stopped train and feeling as if you were moving backward because an express was whizzing past you on the very next track.

"This certainly is a slow form of transportation," Betty Morrison remarked. "Where are we going actually? I mean, do you have any idea at all where we'll come down?"

"Yes," Ted replied. "I do. We're expected at a brunch in the foothills not far from Placitas. You, the governor, the senator, Blake, and the archbishop, that is. You didn't think the balloon fiesta would give champagne to the ground crews and not offer you VIPs any, did you?"

She smiled. "Fun!"

At the PA booth, Lauren joked with the chase crews, many of whom were already a little high on the champagne. Early this morning, back at the beauty ranch, she had rolled each long green bottle in a section of the *Albuquerque Herald* and fitted it into a shoe box. Alongside, she tucked half a dozen foil-wrapped croissants from La Mangerie, a French pastry shop recently opened by some Italians from New York. Without appearing to watch too closely, she tried to keep tabs on the target balloons.

When the *Camelot* popped up, everyone had turned to stare, so she hadn't given away her special interest. Thank heavens Moira made the lift-off, Lauren thought. Now I won't have to babysit.

No one had paid particular attention to the *Windfoal*'s ascent. Now Lauren was watching for the *Artful Dodger*, *Rainbow's End*, or the *Sun Power*.

Although they'd decided Lauren should stay behind—since her name and the name of her business had been broadcast in connection with the champagne brunches—she'd known all along she'd be going . . . one way or another.

Lauren watched Cliff through binoculars. He was in corduroy pants and the same old sheepskin jacket he had been wearing when he walked into Moira's party two nights ago. He was making a systematic inspection of *Rainbow's End*, the balloon in which he would be flying Senator Claridge. Its multicolored fabric rippled as it swayed back and forth.

"Hey, boy," she heard one crew member challenge, "your balloon ever gonna lift off? That's your balloon, ain't it, that ugly piece of plastic?"

"Sure is," the other replied mildly, unzipping his silver windbreaker and taking a generous rinse of champagne. "*Sun Power*, balloon of the future."

"Look at that, will ya," a man said, almost knocking the binoculars out of Lauren's hand as he raised an arm to point. "Boy, howdy!" Everyone looked.

It was an Indian—not just your ordinary, everyday pueblo guy in worn jeans and dusty boots—but a Hollywood Indian in full regalia, an honest-to-goodness chief out of some Saturday matinee.

His face was framed by an elaborate feather headdress that streamed down his back. Red and white streaks were painted on his flat brown cheeks. Strings of brightly colored beads and a heavy turquoise and silver necklace covered the front of the fringed buckskin costume. Over one shoulder, he wore a scarlet Hudson Bay blanket striped with a broad black band.

Lauren could not believe her eyes! Why on earth had Valencio dressed himself up like that? What in the hell was he doing?

She fumbled in her coat pocket for her walkie-talkie. "Gilda calling Solar Bear, Gilda calling Bear," she whispered excitedly.

Rod came in right away. "Bear here, Gilda. Do you see what I see?"

"I see it but I don't believe it!"

"Jesus!"

"What'll we do?"

There was a long pause. "Crazy Fox is no dumbbell. Let's see what he's up to. There's nothing else we can do."

Lauren stood on her toes to get a better view. Valencio was parading through the crowd very slowly, and they loved it! They were backing out of his way to create an open pathway for him and clapping as he passed, one arm upraised. A cameraman darted out in front to catch him for the evening news. The crowd's attention had been diverted momentarily from the big balloons, much as circus goers headed for the main ring are diverted by the side shows.

Joe followed several feet behind his uncle. He looked most unhappy and was plainly hoping no one would know he was connected with that crazy Indian ahead.

Lauren felt herself being swept along by the crowd, which was rapidly getting bigger as people caught sight of Valencio. They began calling questions out to him, but Valencio only stared stoically ahead. The people followed him as if he were some sort of Pied Piper until he came to a stop near a large orange balloon with a zigzag design—the *Artful Dodger!*

There already was a group of people near the *Dodger*, Lauren saw. They were clustered around a downed pilot. A Catholic priest seemed to be sending someone to First Aid Headquarters for help.

Valencio came face to face with the archbishop in two long strides. The Indian raised one buckskin-fringed arm in an exaggerated ceremonial salute. All eyes returned to him at the sound of his voice.

"Big Chief Crazy Fox, me fly white man's wonder ball," he announced loudly, deadpan under the war paint. "Pilot chief, he catchum altitude sickness. Me fly Great White Padre in wonder ball. Great White Padre pray we be safe."

Everyone laughed. Lauren looked over at the archbishop to see his reaction. He made a graceful motion of helplessness with one elegant hand.

"We have not been informed of a change in plan. . ." he began hesitantly, but the crowd was applauding wildly now and drowned out the rest of his soft words. They clearly thought this was part of the show.

Valencio embraced the archbishop and kissed him on both cheeks, leaving streaks of red and white on the clerical face.

"Me fly Great White Padre in wonder ball," he repeated, and before Lauren could believe it was happening, Valencio and Joe had the archbishop in the balloon and they were off. The people on the ground stood applauding, looking up at the odd trio.

It had taken place in the time frame of three or four minutes and had not attracted the attention of a single festival official.

Lauren hurried back to her post at the PA booth. Most of the balloons still on the ground were fully buoyant. Balloons were lifting off everywhere. She guessed there were more than three hundred in the sky now.

She raised the binoculars again, looking for Cliff. Oh, Lord, had *Rainbow's End* taken off while she was watching Valencio perform?

No. Cliff stood near the gondola where Senator Claridge, with a broad smile on his face, was still shaking hands. A little black-clad lady hovered next to the unwary pilot. Suddenly the pilot jumped and clapped a hand to his rump. His cry had been short, muffled by the boisterous noise of the crowd, and he crumpled so quickly most of those around him failed to see it.

Lauren got a close-up of the altar-society lady as she slipped past Cliff. It was Mercedes herself. Mercedes eyed Cliff as if she had never seen him before and walked sedately by, disappearing quietly among the people, a little old Spanish grandmother, anonymous in her typicality.

Lauren focused on Mercedes's victim. The downed pilot was the third balloonist—not counting the service-station attendant—the altar society had done in with their needles. The fallen bodies were so far apart that no one but the raiders was aware that each instance was not an isolated case.

Lauren lowered her glasses. The raid was almost over. *Rainbow's End* was ready to go, and then Rod and the governor would lift off. Less than half the balloons were left on the ground now. The launching field would empty quickly. The big event was almost at an end.

She ran as fast as she could toward *Rainbow's End*, passing one of the launch directors on her way. He was crossing names off his list of entries, balloons that already had received his official lift-off signal.

She leaped over the prone body of the young pilot who lay where Mercedes's needle had dropped him. When her fingers caught hold of the suede-padded rail of the *Rainbow's End*, the balloon already was several inches above the ground. With a hop, she placed her fine fanny firmly on the railing and then jackknifed her legs, swinging them over and planting herself between the two men in the gondola.

"Hey," she said breathlessly, "mind if I join you?"

Cliff smiled broadly. "Hell, no, Lauren, though it may be a case of three's a crowd." He jerked his chin toward Senator Claridge.

"Oh, I'm not that fat!" She laughed, playfully bumping one hip against him and the other against the senator in rapid succession. "There's lots of room!"

"Senator Claridge, have you met Lauren Van Dressler, owner of the Enchanted Door Beauty Ranch?"

"No, I haven't had the pleasure," the passenger replied gallantly, "but I've heard of the Enchanted Door many times from my wife."

Just like his picture, Lauren thought, inspecting him in her frank, friendly way. He had to be sixty, but the years certainly didn't show. He was a big man with large features and intelligent brown eyes. Although his thick hair had already turned gray, the sideburns were still dark. His body was well-proportioned and by its very size gave the impression of strength and masculinity. He wore the Zia symbol bolo tie that was his personal signature both in Washington and his home town of Las Cruces.

"Hi!" Lauren said warmly. She was conscious that he was inspecting her as she had inspected him. "Have you ever been up in a balloon before, Senator?"

The twinkle in his eyes was definitely sexy. "No, I can't say that I have," he replied in the deep voice for which he was famous. "But I think I'm going to enjoy it very much!"

As they smiled at each other, his big hands were fumbling in pockets too small for them and finally produced a pipe, pouch, and some matches. He hunched his shoulders and took his time lighting the pipe. After taking a few experimental puffs, he laid his head back and stretched like a great jungle cat.

"What a treat it is to have the pressure off," he sighed. "It's so peaceful up here. It's great knowing no reporters are going to turn up to ask embarrassing questions. I can use some time to recharge my motor."

The three of them looked over the side, watching balloons rise all around them in an explosion of color.

"The whole world's having a birthday party!" Lauren laughed. Both men smiled at her.

Lauren glanced from one handsome face to the other as they floated along in the brightening sunlight, not saying anything or feeling the need to. She was just plain enjoying being up in the sky with not one but two terrific men.

Rod watched *Rainbow's End* glide over the trees at the end of the field. Every one of his raiders was airborne. Unless he messed up, the first phase of their plan would be a success. Now if the governor would just get his ass over here!

Rod looked around for him, thinking how well the hijack had gone so far in the confusion of milling crowds. Would anyone have believed four dignitaries could be kidnapped right under the eyes of several thousand spectators!

But number five was the prime target: the governor. Number five would be the trickiest. The crowd was thinning. If Kate spotted him . . .

He looked at Kate. She was standing by the *Sun Power* talking with the volunteers who had replaced her crew. He saw an older woman carrying a large black purse approach his ex-wife.

Kate sagged to the ground. People bent over her.

"What happened?"

"She fainted!"

"All of a sudden, she just keeled over!"

". . . the damndest thing!"

Rod slid the mirror glasses into his pocket and pulled off the stocking cap. He pushed past the curious bystanders.

"Hey! What happened to my wife?" he cried. He went down on his knees and shook her by the shoulders. "Kate—Kate—" He felt for her pulse.

Rod spread his hands helplessly, looking up at the circle of faces. "I've got to take her to first aid," he said. He picked her up, shaking his head at a guy who offered to help. "No, thanks, I can manage." He walked off with her.

She seemed heavier than he remembered. He moved sideways into the narrow space between the VW bus and the metallic blue custom van. He opened the van's sliding door and laid her beside the pilot of the *Artful Dodger*, both sunk in a sea of blue shag.

"Sleep warm," he murmured.

Rod peered around the corner of the van. A group of festival officials had collected at the *Sun Power*. He knew their problem: no one knew exactly how to fly the solar balloon.

He forced himself to wait several minutes. Then he ducked out and started back toward the *Sun Power*. At last a public relations man recognized him and dashed over, grabbing onto his arm.

"Hey, Riley, listen, *you've* got to fly the governor!" The man's eyes bulged with excitement. Almost as an afterthought, he asked, "Kate's okay, isn't she?"

Pretending reluctance, Rod let himself be propelled along toward the *Sun Power*. I couldn't have asked for a better setup, he thought.

Aloud he said, "She'll be all right. It's probably that flu going around. I heard another pilot got sick . . ."

The impatient PR man jumped in front of Rod, bringing them both to a dead stop.

"Riley, for Chrissakes, you're the only one we know besides Kate who can fly the *Sun Power*! We've got three national networks waiting to film the sun-state governor in a solar balloon!"

Hands almost lifted Rod into the gondola.

"Good morning, Governor," he said cordially. "I'm Rodriguez Riley, your pilot." He stuck out his hand and grasped the governor's.

"Glad to know you, Rodriguez," Cortés replied. "I'm sorry the young lady has been taken ill. They tell me she's getting medical attention."

"She's doing well," Rod replied.

"Well, let's get underway," the governor said. "I've got to be back in Santa Fe for a one-thirty meeting."

In the southeast corner of the balloon field, a short, bald man in brown corduroy leaned against the flagpole flying the U.S. and New Mexico flags. His eyes moved constantly, inspecting everyone in the immediate area.

He waited until a woman using one of the back-to-back telephones finished her conversation. Then he flipped away what was left of his smoke and moved in with the correct coins ready. He lowered his head, cupping his free hand around his lips as he spoke. It was a short call.

"Mr. Brunalesci, please. Boss? This is Tige. That party we were worried about—the one with the '47 Ford truck? Well, he, uh, he never came back to his truck, but he was here in Albuquerque, after all . . .

"No, I didn't get that lucky. . . Now, wait a minute! He's up in a goddam balloon! And, get this, boss, Governor Cortés is in the balloon with him!"

There was a brief pause during which the man closed his eyes and moved his hand over his forehead.

"Yeah, well, uh . . ." Tige said, "they gotta come down sometime, don't they? Okay, so I hang around."

SIX

The bent old lady stood for a few moments gazing apprehensively at the tall building. Then she patted her purse with a gesture of finality and, clutching the handrail, made her way a step at a time up the long flight.

Her heart beat rapidly. Thank the Holy Virgin she'd found the building. She'd wanted to be sure she would not be late; the buses were not always reliable. She would deliver the letter now instead of waiting until noon as Mercedes had instructed. Surely, it would not matter.

The pretty girl at the front desk of the *Albuquerque Herald* was admiring her new eyelashes in a tiny round mirror with a picture of a four-leaf clover on the back. She was so engrossed with her image that it was quite a while before she became aware of the elderly Spanish lady waiting patiently on the opposite side of the counter.

"Oh, can I help you?" she asked.

"I have something for the editor," the lady said nervously, looking around her.

"Yes?" The girl held out her hand.

"It is something very private and personal, very important," the old woman explained with an apologetic smile.

"Of course."

The Spanish lady fumbled with the clasp of her big purse. Her small hands, encased in black cotton gloves, shakily withdrew a long white envelope.

"You will give this to the editor yourself, only to him?" she persisted, looking directly into the false eyelashes.

"Certainly. As soon as he comes in this morning."

"Gracias. Vaya con Dios."

The envelope changed hands and the outer door closed behind the old woman. The receptionist looked at the words "Señor Editor" on the envelope and smiled. She put the envelope into a cubbyhole under the desk and returned to her mirror.

Several minutes later, as the girl was applying a second coat of lacquer to her long fingernails, she saw the editor coming down the hall. He was reading some papers he had clutched in his hand and almost passed by her desk without looking up. Suddenly he sniffed suspiciously, but before he could say anything about the fresh nail polish, she waved her "Gypsy Plum" talons vaguely in the direction of the cubbyhole and said, "Someone left something for you." He reached into the cubbyhole, scowling. "That stuff stinks."

"An old lady," she said, unperturbed. "One of our senior citizens. A chicana."

He looked at the envelope addressed "Señor Editor."

"Another letter to the editor," he grumbled. "Any other mail?"

"The mailman just came a few minutes ago," said the girl, searching through the piles of papers on her desk. She casually slid the page with the half-done crossword puzzle under a heap of papers. She was careful to use only the balls of her fingertips so as not to smear the manicure.

"I had the mail right here," she said, frowning. "Oops, it must have slid off the desk into the wastebasket." She leaned forward, her slender fingers hovering above the wastebasket's contents.

"Never mind," the editor said impatiently. "I'll get it myself."

He reached down and grabbed the stack of envelopes with one beefy hand. With the other hand still holding the "Señor Editor" envelope between his thumb and forefinger, he adjusted the rimless glasses that had slipped precariously to the end of his nose. He glared at the receptionist and walked back to his office.

Without taking off his coat, he began thumbing through the return addresses until his fingers felt something soft. A damp cotton ball smudged with purplish nail polish was stuck between two envelopes. He threw the handful of envelopes on his desk top in disgust and headed for the city room.

From a thousand feet above the Rio Grande Valley the river was a shiny ribbon carelessly strung through the bare branches of the twisted old cottonwoods. The sun was now well above the mountain, shooting its friendly rays against the silver surface of the *Sun Power*. All of the balloons were up now, sailing through the turquoise skies like galleons nudged by gentle winds.

Beneath the *Sun Power*, Rod could see thousands of cars leaving the balloon field to slowly thread their way south back to the city. Traffic northbound was light, and an ambulance with flashing red lights streaked down the freeway toward the field.

Rod looked at his passenger in the yellow parka. The governor seemed preoccupied with his own private thoughts. The hard hat covered his high forehead and rested on the aviator sunglasses he wore. Only the bottom half of Cortés's face was visible: the prominent cheekbones, aquiline nose, and proud jaw. Cortés looked less a governor than the construction worker he'd once been.

But governor he was. The lean hispano from northern New Mexico had worked his way through college doing construction work. As his youthful body hardened, so had his ambition. He began by selling real estate. At twenty-five he had his own agency, then ran for the state senate two years later. As a businessman climbs the corporate ladder, Cortés mounted the state's political system. At thirty-five he ran for governor, shrewdly appealing to public distrust of special interests. He promised to protect the state's energy resources and prevent New Mexico from becoming a dumping ground for the nation's wastes. He promised to destroy the syndicate's drug pipeline from Mexico. Now, just one year in office and one of the youngest governors in the country, *Time* and *Newsweek* had named Cortés a "comer."

Cortés shifted slightly, apparently aware of Rod's observation.

"What the hell is that?" he asked, squinting eastward into the sun. "It looks like toilet paper."

Pieces of pink tissue fluttered from an ocher-colored balloon floating just east of the *Sun Power*.

Rod grinned. "The pilot dropped toilet paper over the side to test wind direction below."

"How do you test the wind direction above?"

"The only way is to go up."

Cortés stared up into the *Sun Power*'s envelope. The sunshine was bright through the clear plastic half of the balloon.

"How come nobody else knew how to fly this balloon?"

"Well, Governor, it's my balloon. I built it."

"What's so different about it?"

"That clear plastic up there, that's what's so different," Rod said. "You see, the clear side is the window half and the silver is the reflector half. The silver part is lined with black. The sun shines through the plastic lens onto the black and heats the air inside."

Cortés nodded. "Clever."

"Better than clever, Governor. The *Sun Power* can revolutionize ballooning. In this state, ballooning could be more than a sport. New Mexico could lead the way in using balloons for commercial transport. Solar balloons could carry large lightweight loads free."

"Yes," Cortés said with interest, "that certainly would conserve fuel."

"Right," Rod said. "Propane is the biggest expense in flying a balloon. But with a solar balloon, you can stay up as long as the sun shines. Propane is just a backup for cloudy days."

"Yes, very interesting," the governor said.

"Solar energy can be used in the same way on the ground, Governor," Rod went on. "There are low-tech, inexpensive ways to use sunshine for free and depend on expensive forms of energy only as a backup. We can—"

The governor was looking at his watch.

"Good," Cortés said, "let's make it a point to talk. I'm sorry, I'm not able to keep my mind on it now. I'm interested, though, in hearing what you have to say. I take it that's your line of work?"

"My papers say solar engineer, but I'm a jack of all trades."

Cortés smiled. "Look, I hate to be so edgy, but I've got a very important meeting right after lunch. It's one I've been hoping for for a long time. It'll clean up this state."

You bet it will, Rod thought.

The editor wearily returned from his weekly meeting with the publisher at the country club. God, he hated Saturdays. Bad enough the ritual brunch with the boss. But Saturday was always a slow news day. Barring a plane crash or another eruption in the Middle East, nobody made news on Saturday.

He sat at his polished wood desk, leaned back in the leather swivel chair, and allowed himself a belch. He bent down and opened the bottom desk drawer revealing a bottle of Chivas Regal, two smudged glasses, three swizzle sticks, a package of plastic spoons, and three bottles of Gelusil. He looked longingly at the Chivas but grabbed a bottle of Gelusil.

He scanned the first edition of the *Albuquerque Bugle*. Not much there. On Saturdays, even the fierce competition between the morning *Herald* and the afternoon *Bugle* seemed to subside. They'd each just fill up the front page with whatever they could get. He tossed the paper into the waste basket.

The mail was spread before him. Monday's editorial on the slowness of garbage pickups remained half-written in the typewriter. His big thumb rubbed the bridge of his nose where the heavy black eyebrows met. "Can't face it now," he muttered. He picked up the phone to call city desk.

"Smitty, what have you got cityside for page one?" the editor's voice boomed.

"No banner headline but lots of color. Start of the balloon fiesta. Photographer got some nice shots at the mass ascension. Hundreds of balloons in the air at once."

"Who've you got covering it?"

"The new kid."

The editor groaned. "Not the eager one who wears the trench coat?"

"The very one," the city editor chuckled. "Our own Clark Kent."

"Well, we may have to lead with the balloons. What else do you have?"

"Nothing better. A wrapup of the legislative session—the political reporter did a pretty good analysis of the sunshine tax. Another story on the flu epidemic."

"The flu's pretty warmed over for front page. Unless there's a new angle on it?"

"Kid said four people passed out at the balloon fiesta. First-aid station thought it was the flu. Sent them to the hospital."

"Kid check with the hospital to confirm it's the flu?"

"Told him to. He should be calling back to report."

"Well, let me know what develops."

The pine trees sprang out of the mountainside in unnaturally straight rows, reminding Rod of the boar bristle hairbrush his grandmother occasionally used to apply to his backside.

Now, leaning over the side of the *Sun Power*, Rod could smell the sharpness of the young trees, an almost painfully green sensation. The raiders' balloons clustered at the same level in the sky above the forested foothills.

"Hey, where're we going?" the governor asked. "Most of the balloons are heading south. Looks like they're flying back to Albuquerque."

"Well, as I was telling you before, Governor," Rod replied amiably, "balloons don't always stay together. They catch different air currents and go different ways."

Cortés looked intently at the closest balloon. He frowned. "Isn't that the lieutenant governor in that green and gray balloon?"

"I know it's the *Windfoal*," Rod said helpfully, "but I don't know who the woman is."

"Give me your binoculars, please."

"Yeah, uh, just a sec," Rod stalled. He looked through the binoculars himself, focusing on the terrain below. "Sometimes you can see wildlife in these mountains from up here," he began. The binoculars were yanked out of his hands, the strap snapped taut around his neck, and he was dragged as if on a leash.

Cortés was sighting on the *Windfoal*. "It is Betty," he muttered. He turned the glasses on the second balloon in the cluster. "Senator Claridge. . ." The glasses moved again and then again. He dropped the binoculars. They snapped abruptly back and hit Rod's chest. Cortés glared at him.

"What the hell's going on here, Riley? There's a politico in every damn one of these balloons. Are you asking me to believe that's a coincidence?"

Rod swallowed. "Well, it was supposed to be a surprise, Governor. The festival officials arranged for us to take you down in a mountain meadow for a champagne brunch."

"*Brunch*? Nobody said anything about a *brunch*!"

"I told you it was a surprise."

"That's out! I don't have time for any brunch. I thought I made it clear that I have to be in Santa Fe at one-thirty. That means we have to get back to Albuquerque before noon. Take me back!"

"But my friends and I thought—"

"Your friends?" The governor's eyes narrowed suspiciously. "I thought you said the festival officials planned this picnic."

Rod hesitated several seconds. "The officials are my friends," he said finally.

"Take me back," the governor insisted.

"I'm sorry, Governor Cortés, but I can't do that. I have my orders."

"Damn your orders! I'm the governor of this state. I don't know who you got your instructions from, but I'm *ordering* you to take me back to Albuquerque."

"Hold your horses, Governor. It's not even nine o'clock yet. We'll be landing in a few minutes."

The governor stared at him a moment, a nervous tic starting up by his left eye. He turned away rudely. Rod could see the knuckles go white as the governor's long fingers gripped the rim of the gondola.

The two men fell into a hostile silence.

The pile of letters to the editor was spread before him. There was no putting it off. This was the editor's least favorite job—picking the letters that would appear in the next day's column.

He began halfheartedly tearing open the envelopes. Two letters on slow garbage pickup. Good, that fit in with his editorial. One letter demanding recall of the mayor for refusing to fund a department to contact unidentified flying objects; one penciled message—on chartreuse paper yet— objecting to the editorial on Afghanistan.

The phone rang and the editor gratefully picked it up. "Yeah?"

"Smitty here. The kid just called in from the hospital about those people who collapsed at the balloon fiesta. He was so excited, I could hardly understand him."

"What'd he say? They conscious yet? They have the flu?"

"The answer's no to your last two questions. That's the weird part. Doctors aren't sure, but they suspect drugs."

"Dopers? Maybe got a bad batch?"

"Naw, don't think so. Doctors said no needle tracks on their arms. More likely they were drugged. Kid says witnesses claim they just keeled over. Doctors think it sounds like a fast-acting barbiturate."

"Any connection between the four?"

"Three of them were pilots scheduled to take up dignitaries in balloons today. Don't know anything about the fourth—he's a gas-station attendant."

"Who were the pilots scheduled to take up?"

"The archbishop, lieutenant governor, and Senator Claridge."

"So what happened?"

"The senator, lieutenant governor, and archbishop were taken up by substitute pilots."

"You say the governor's pilot was okay?"

"Far as I know, the governor's balloon went up as scheduled."

"Hmmm. The senator's pilot, the lieutenant governor's pilot, the archbishop's pilot—that's funny—and a service-station attendant. Interesting coincidence—if it is a coincidence. Keep me posted."

The bright-orange *Artful Dodger* made a dramatic splash in the cloudless sky above the green pine trees and snow-covered granite foothills. From its gondola, the archbishop could see for miles. The tumbled boulders, the escarpment lifting sheer to the blue heights, the evergreens, reminded him of his native Switzerland. He had been appalled at his appointment to this wasteland of sagebrush, juniper, and arid stretches of desert. He had never felt at ease in the vast, stark landscape. Now, looking into the forest and imagining spring green grass, yellow primroses, blue lupine, and snowdrops, he smiled.

The flight over the mountains had been tranquil. His companions had been silent for the most part, which had relieved the archbishop. He'd been afraid the painted Indian would continue his bizarre behavior. But in the sky the old man became suddenly taciturn.

Beneath the balloon lay two clearings—white meadows separated by thick woods. A little farther beyond them, the land dropped unexpectedly into a deep, craggy canyon. As they passed over the smallest clearing, some unusual conical shadows on the snow made Grignard look more closely.

At the edge of the clearing was a cluster of tipis. A large one, surrounded by five smaller ones, streamers and feathers hanging motionless from the poles that protruded from the top of each. They appeared to be made of dark hides, but here and there were painted symbols, generally weathered in tone.

At the opposite side of the meadow was an unpainted barn, several shacks and motley outbuildings.

"Are those tipis?" Grignard asked Joe.

Joe nodded. "We're going to land in the larger clearing beyond this one," he volunteered, "for the champagne brunch."

The archbishop caught sight of a yellow school bus in the farther clearing and nodded politely, but he was fascinated by the site below.

The more Grignard looked, the more apparent it became that the place was deserted. He studied it curiously. As the balloon drifted closer he could read the peeling paint on a large sign leaning against the barn that read: ONLY ONE DOLLAR TO HAVE YOUR PICTURE TAKEN WITH A REAL INDIAN. Nearby was the wreckage of an old buckboard missing a wheel, on which was lettered: GET YOUR SNAX HERE. COKE. FRIED BREAD. SNO CONES. Two wooden outhouses stood sentry at the edge of the meadow opposite the tipis. Between them a crudely lettered sign pointed to a grove of young pines: CUT YOUR OWN XMAS TREE $25.

"What is this place?" the archbishop asked.

"Movie set," Joe said.

"They're not still. . .?" Grignard began.

"Nope, it's abandoned."

"The tipis are part of the set?"

Joe nodded. "They're authentic replicas. The poles are set in concrete," he explained, "so they wouldn't tip over during filming sequence. The hides are nailed to the poles—they'll be there long after the rest of the buildings have rotted away."

Grignard found America ironic. Hollywood probably had spent more for this set than today's Native American could afford to spend for his own home.

"Whose is it now?"

"I lease it," Valencio said.

Grignard stared at him. "I needed a tax break," Valencio went on, his face serious beneath the war paint, the feathers in his headdress fluttering majestically. "But if I don't watch it, the place makes a profit."

The archbishop gave a courteous nod. He thought, Indians 10, Church 0.

Valencio winked solemnly at the archbishop. "Time we go down. Great White Padre pray!"

Joe pulled on the ripcord. Nothing happened. He pulled again. Still nothing happened. Worriedly, he peered up to the roof of the balloon and yanked hard. The deflation panel gave and the balloon dropped rapidly.

"Whoa!" yelled Rod from the *Sun Power*. "Give her some gas!"

Joe grabbed the burner handle with his other hand, still clutching the ripcord. The balloon bobbed erratically. Valencio, impassive, hands resting lightly on the rim of the gondola, viewed the ground. The archbishop, his face as white as his hair, braced himself with both hands on the superstructure. The silver cross set with turquoise bounced against his chest each time the balloon bobbed.

"Mon Dieu!" Grignard gasped.

"Holy horse turds!" yelped Joe.

Joe's perspiring hand slipped off the burner handle, and the balloon dropped suddenly. Joe lurched and tried to right himself by grabbing the ripline with both hands.

The passengers of the *Windfoal, Camelot,* and *Rainbow's End* watched with horror as the orange balloon streaked down from the sky. Rod covered his face with his hands.

The bottom of the gondola slammed into the leaky roof of the shack marked MENS. Sounds of rotten wood splintering filled the air. The *Artful Dodger*'s gondola then bounced to the ground, tipped over, and dumped its human contents.

Joe was first to his feet. He extended a hand to the shaken archbishop. "You okay, Padre?"

Grignard opened his eyes carefully. "By some miracle," he murmured.

Valencio got to his feet slowly. He looked Joe straight in the eye. "*Artful Dodger,* my ass."

Time seemed suspended for the trio in the multistriped *Rainbow's End* following the demise of the *Artful Dodger.* They had watched in silence as the three men climbed out of the wicker basket amid the splintered wood of the destroyed outhouse.

"They seem to be all right," the senator said finally.

"That bonkers kid," Cliff said, shaking his head.

Lauren remained silent. She clung to Cliff's left arm, her long nails digging into his sheepskin coat. Her face was pale. The expertly applied tawny blusher now made her cheeks look oddly striped, as if she were a small girl who had dabbled in mommy's makeup.

"Let's go down," said Cliff.

Lauren let go of Cliff to brace herself against the basket's railing. Cliff smiled at her reassuringly.

"Don't worry, Lauren," he said. "We're going on over to the big meadow. I'll make it a smooth landing. Bend your knees a little when we touch down. You too, Senator, to cushion the bump."

The *Rainbow's End* floated over the tipi village where the

orange and yellow *Artful Dodger* lay limply on one side. At the big meadow Cliff set the balloon down gently in the powdered snow. The senator straightened up and turned to Lauren.

"Are you all right now, my dear?" he asked.

Still crouched slightly, she muttered, "So far."

One more letter to go.

The editor absently tore off the end of the envelope marked "Señor Editor." He upended the envelope and gave it one fast shake. A small piece of white paper folded down the middle slid out of the envelope onto the desk. The editor was about to unfold it when the telephone rang. It was Smitty.

"Something's fishy. Two more drugged pilots have been found. One's the woman who was going to take up the governor. Named Kate Riley. She and another pilot—the guy scheduled to take up Commissioner Blake—were dumped unconscious into the back of a van at the balloon field. She just came to, madder than hell. Claims her ex-husband stole her balloon, the *Sun Power*—it's the solar balloon."

"She say what happened?" the editor asked. He nervously toyed with the white piece of paper on his desk, running his thumb along the fold.

"Said she was just standing by her balloon getting ready to take up the governor, felt a sharp pain in the ass, and blacked out. Woke up in the back of the van with some unconscious stranger."

"She thinks her ex-husband took the balloon—*and* the governor?"

"Yeah, and witnesses say so, too."

"Is the mass ascension over yet?" The editor's voice was excited.

"All the balloons are back but the ones carrying the dignitaries."

There was a nervous silence.

"Let's see." The editor began counting his fingers. "You

have the governor, a city commissioner, lieutenant governor, senator and the archbishop—all up in the air with unscheduled pilots. . ." The editor's fingers brushed the piece of white paper on his desk. It flipped open.

His eyes involuntarily went to the paper. In black ink, block print, upper case, he read:

TO THE PEOPLE OF NEW MEXICO AND THE UNITED STATES:

WE ARE HOLDING GOVERNOR CORTÉS, LIEUTENANT GOVERNOR MORRISON, SENATOR CLARIDGE, CITY COMMISSIONER BLAKE, AND ARCHBISHOP GRIGNARD TO PROTEST THE SUNSHINE TAX.

WHEN A GOVERNMENT ILLEGITIMATELY INTERPOSES ITSELF BETWEEN A FREE PEOPLE AND OUR GREAT NATURAL SOURCE OF POWER, IGNORES THE PUBLIC GOOD IN FAVOR OF VESTED INTERESTS, AND EXHIBITS CONTEMPT FOR THE GOVERNED BY OPENLY MANIPULATING THE LEGISLATIVE PROCESSES, THAT PEOPLE MUST TAKE SWIFT AND DECISIVE ACTION TO DEFEND THEIR LIBERTY.

WE ARE HOLDING HOSTAGES TO DEMONSTRATE AGAINST THE SUNSHINE TAX. WE HAVE NO WEAPONS AND WILL NOT HARM THEM IN ANY WAY.

WE ASK ALL AMERICANS TO JOIN US IN OUR PROTEST AND DEMAND REPEAL OF THE SUNSHINE TAX. FELLOW AMERICANS, WE STILL HAVE REDRESS AGAINST NONREPRESENTATIVE GOVERNMENT. USE IT. CONTACT YOUR LEGISLATOR AND INSIST ON GOVERNMENT BY CONSENT. SUNSHINE SHOULD BE FREE!

"Oh, no!" the editor moaned. He dropped the receiver on his desk and reread the note.

"Are you there, boss? You there?" came Smitty's voice from the fallen receiver.

The editor glanced at the clock.

"Oh, Christ," he groaned, his head in his hands. "The story of the decade and it breaks on *Bugle* time."

Moira had watched the *Artful Dodger*'s crash open-mouthed. Her heart still pounded in her ears even after she saw the passengers scramble, apparently unharmed, out of the overturned gondola. She looked frantically for Ted's balloon, the *Windfoal*. With relief she saw it drift over to the big meadow and make a smooth landing a hundred yards from the *Rainbow's End*. The bus was parked nearby, its wooden doors open in the back. On the ground, Lauren and Serefina were rolling up the deflated balloons as Cliff and the senator dragged the gondolas through the snow toward the bus.

Now the *Camelot* and the *Sun Power* were the only balloons aloft.

Rod's waiting for me to land, Moira thought. She looked down into the meadow and then with disgust at the sleeping commissioner, propped in the corner of the triangular basket. She had outfoxed herself with the brandy. He would be no help.

Moira gave the ripcord a tentative pull. The line resisted, then whipped out of her gloved hands. With a sinking feeling, she realized she wouldn't be strong enough to pull the ripcord and land by herself. The line was far too short to give her leverage.

She bit her thin lips and tugged nervously at the red wool muffler around her neck. The muffler!

She gave the burner handle one short blast to buy herself more time. As the balloon ascended, she yanked off the muffler. She removed the bulky gloves and held them between her teeth. Now she carefully tied the end of the muffler to the ripcord. The muffler lengthened the ripcord by six feet.

She nudged Blake with her boot. His unconscious body slid down toward her sideways in the fetal position, his head still upright in the corner. She bent down and straightened his body, positioning the feet opposite his head.

She lifted the bulky torso a few inches, sliding the muffler underneath. She would use him for extra weight on the ripline. If the knot held, it should work. Her legs straddled Blake. She peered over the edge of the gondola, then gave the end of the muffler a tug. The commissioner's body rolled slightly. "Please, God," she whispered, "make it work."

From the *Sun Power* above the meadow, Rod had watched the *Camelot* shoot up in the air and then drop down just as quickly. Now he could see only the top of Moira's dark head and the flapping of what appeared to be a strip of red cloth attached to the ripcord. The balloon with the red St. George's cross was dropping quickly toward the thick trees at the edge of the big meadow.

"What's she doing?" asked the governor.

Rod only shook his head, his eyes never leaving the Camelot.

"Is she alone in that balloon?"

"Might as well be," Rod replied.

The two watched silently as the *Camelot* slashed downward into the pines. The sound of breaking branches and scratching needles accompanied Moira's screams. The basket bounced on top of the trees, two heads popping above the gondola's rim with each bounce. At last the brutal bouncing stopped.

"Do you suppose they're okay?" the governor asked in a low voice.

"Get me out of here, Teddy!" a female voice screamed from the tree.

"They're okay," grinned Rod, and landed the *Sun Power* smoothly and uneventfully less than one hundred feet from the tree that entangled *Camelot*. He jumped over the side of the gondola and, without breaking pace, ran toward the treed balloon. The yellow bus was speeding across the meadow toward the *Camelot*. Rod was first to the tree. The others piled out of the bus.

"Get me out of here," Moira screamed again.

The drunken commissioner slowly got to his feet.

"Where are we?" he asked in a woozy voice.

Moira gave him a bitter glance.

"Up a tree," she said.

The governor watched the commotion at the west edge of the meadow. He swung himself stealthily over the side of the gondola and made a sudden dash east for the woods. If he could cover the two hundred yards undetected, he might escape.

"Hey, Juan, where're you going?" Betty Morrison called after him. Cortés ran faster. His breathing was so light that he could hear someone running after him. He resisted the urge to look back.

"Cortés!" Rod shouted. Now the governor glanced over his shoulder. Rod's long legs were closing the gap between them. Cortés ran harder. His leather-soled boots were slipping badly in the melting snow. Suddenly his right foot skidded out from under him as it glanced off a hidden boulder. His leg folded underneath him as Rod lunged. Rod landed on top of him, forcing the air out of his lungs.

"Arahumph!" the governor gasped. The others ran toward the two men piled on the ground. "Get offa me, *pendejo*," Cortés growled. Rod slowly got up.

The governor struggled to his knees; his yellow parka was caked with mud and snow. He tried to stand, then grimaced and grabbed at his ankle.

"What are you two doing?" came Betty's sarcastic voice. "Playing a little touch football?"

With effort, Cortés rose to his lanky six feet and faced her.

"You fool," he snarled, his eyes narrow slits. "We've been hijacked!"

Serefina pushed past the angry governor. She grabbed Rod's wet sleeve, pulling him away from the others.

"Our note was delivered early," she told him in a low voice. "It just came over the radio."

An uneasy look flickered in Rod's eyes. "Too soon, too soon. They'll be sending out planes.

"We've got to hurry," Rod told the others. "Get that balloon down out of the tree. Put the camouflage tarpaulin on the bus and let's load the balloons. Ted, the snow has to look like it did before we landed. Cut some pine boughs and brush out all our tracks. Things are moving faster than we planned."

The crowded bus was filled with the smell of damp clothes and cold sweat as it jolted along the old logging road toward tipi village. The hostages were wedged between the gondolas, packed two on each side. The raiders watched from the corners of the bus.

Cortés stood with his back braced against the wall, the gondola of the *Windfoal* pinning him in on one side, *Camelot* on the other. Betty Morrison had been directed to stand in front of him, balancing herself with one arm on each basket. With every bump in the road, she fell against Cortés. The commissioner had been dumped unceremoniously into the *Camelot* basket. He was asleep again, having consumed an entire thermos of ninety-proof Napoleon brandy, and snored damply.

Opposite them, Senator Claridge was crowded between two baskets. He looked grim as he stared at the drooling commissioner.

Rod stood at the back of the bus, legs apart. He looked at their nervous faces and moved slowly among the gondolas.

"Look," he said, "don't be afraid. This isn't a *real* hijacking. It's a peaceful protest. We have no guns, no weapons. We're holding you to protest the sunshine tax. You won't be harmed."

"The *sunshine tax*?" Betty Morrison was incredulous. "You hijacked us because of the *sunshine tax*?"

"We have to undo what you've done, Lieutenant Governor. We hope there will be enough popular support to convince the governor to call a special session of the legislature to repeal the sunshine tax." Rod looked at the governor. Cortés's eyes were black with hostility.

"I don't perform state duties off in the mountains, under duress," the governor replied stiffly. "I discuss these matters in my office in the capitol—and only after you've gone through proper channels."

"You sure weren't available to talk when the tax was passed," Ted commented from the corner.

"I refuse to bargain with a gang of hijackers," Cortés said. He retreated into the yellow parka and watched Rod in rebellious silence.

"You're full of crap," Betty Morrison said to Rod. "If you just wanted to convince the governor, why did you grab the rest of us? Take me back to Cutter Field immediately!"

Rod ignored her.

"Why *did* you take all of us?" the senator asked mildly.

"A bigger splash," said Rod.

"Ah, yes, publicity. I assume you left a ransom note somewhere?"

Rod nodded. "With the newspapers. It says we won't harm you—and we're holding you to gain sufficient support to repeal the sunshine tax."

"What group are you with?" Betty Morrison demanded. "What movement?"

Rod shook his head. "None," he said. Then he met her eyes. "Everyone's."

"Ah," said the senator. "So you're taking your case to the people?"

"Exactly."

"You know you don't have a prayer of getting away with this without being caught. Police will be combing the state looking for us."

"We know."

"But it's worth the prospect of going to jail?"

"Yes, if it comes to that, because the long-term consequences of not taking action are worse than what might happen to us now."

"Say no more," said the senator. He laughed—a large, hearty guffaw that boomed through the bus. "You sound like I did when I was a freshman in Washington."

"This insane plan will never work," snapped Betty Morrison. "You'll rot in jail."

Senator Claridge turned to Betty. "Don't be too sure of that, my dear. Since Watergate, the people have looked with suspicion on the likes of you and me. If their plan works, and it just might, they'll be folk heroes." He gestured toward Cortés. "Not even old stiff-necked Juan here would be so politically foolish as to prosecute them then."

The lieutenant governor's mouth hung open. The governor watched Rod sullenly. Rod looked at Cortés, then at the senator. Claridge was smiling.

"A brilliant plan," the senator said. "Amateurish, but artful. I have just one more question."

"Shoot," said Rod.

"When this is all over, will you handle my reelection campaign?"

Everyone but Cortés and Betty Morrison laughed at Claridge's remark. Cortés stared suspiciously at Rod, his mouth set.

The Our Lady of Sorrows Parish bus rocked along. The old logging road was so overgrown it was little more than a trail shaded by tall trees. Serefina's brows knit in concentration as she steered the bus along the twisting road. The frayed end of the rope securing the camouflage tarp to the top of the bus dangled in front of her. With each jolt the rope swung across the windshield like a wiper. Soon she maneuvered the creaking bus into a graveled area that had been used for tourist parking. A cluster of tipis loomed before them.

The passengers peered out the bus windows. Beyond the tipis, across a small clearing, was a tilting barn and two Chic Sales outhouses. Not much remained standing of the one marked MENS. Spread out on the ground was the *Artful Dodger*.

"Good Lord!" Betty Morrison exclaimed. "An Indian chief and a token priest. You people thought of everything!"

Joe and Valencio squatted there in the midst of the splintered wood, inspecting the orange material. Valencio looked up. The red and white streaks on his face were now smeared with dirt. Several feathers were missing from the elaborate headdress. The archbishop sat peacefully on a large rock nearby, both hands on the silver cross.

"Give me a hand with these blankets and sleeping 'bags, will you, Ted?" Serefina said from the front of the bus. "I guess it will be easier to get some of this stuff out this way because of those gondolas. Lauren, will you and Moira help grandmother unload the kitchen supplies?" She looked for Rod. "Where shall we . . ."

Rod had jumped down from the back of the bus. "Everyone okay?" he called to the Indian men.

Valencio nodded once.

Rod made an okay sign with his thumb and finger. He inspected the tipis one after another while the others dragged gear out onto the ground. "Listen everyone," he said. "This tent will be headquarters for food. Put our catalytic heater in this big tipi, Cliff. We can all sleep in there very comfortably, I think. Now, if you'll please step inside, Miss Morrison, Governor, Senator, Your Excellency. . ." He smiled. "Joe, will you help Commissioner Blake out of that basket?"

At nine-thirty—just one hour and a half after lift-off at Cutter Field—everyone was seated on the rug-covered floor of the big tipi holding hot mugs of coffee provided by Mercedes from a large thermos. Joe carried the transistor radio in and turned it on. After hearing a few words of the newscast, the governor leaned forward tensely. Senator Claridge took his pipe from his mouth, and Betty shushed them all loudly. The archbishop and the commissioner were slower to react. All the hijackers were staring at the small transistor in fascination, straining to hear through the static:

. . . note delivered to the *Albuquerque Herald* from the hijackers claims the hijacking is a political protest. In lieu of a ransom, the hijackers are demanding repeal of the sunshine tax. They claim they are unarmed. Secretary of State Carmen Castillo, now acting governor, said she has every confidence in State Security Chief Hans Daggett, who is in charge of the search and rescue efforts. Daggett could not be reached for comment.

"Then it's true," the commissioner said dazedly. "We are hijacked!"

"Well, well," Claridge said, scratching the side of his nose with his pipe. "We'll have to await developments."

"Wait!" Betty Morrison exploded. "If we have to wait for Carmen Castillo and Hans Daggett, we'll be here till hell freezes over!"

About noon the late-model Plymouth drew up in front of La Hacienda Restaurant in Albuquerque. Brunalesci stepped out from beneath the portal and greeted the bulldog-faced driver who merely nodded, shifting his cigar in his teeth.

"I appreciate your coming down from Santa Fe, Hans," Brunalesci said. "I think it's easier to meet here without being noticed."

Daggett raised his eyebrows. "Where to?"

"Park here, around the plaza somewhere."

"Here? In Old Town?"

"Sure, here in Old Town! This would be the last place either of us would see anyone we know. It's dead after Christmas, even the tourists are gone. We can walk around the plaza."

Daggett threw his stogie butt into the gutter and strolled along casually beside Brunalesci, peeling the cellophane off a fresh cigar. He put the cigar in his mouth but didn't light it.

Brunalesci said, "Tige saw the governor in a balloon with this Riley character, and you can bet they're meeting Bernie somewhere. This whole hijack has got to be a cover-up. I mean, they've really thought of all the angles. No one's going to get hurt; just a political protest—in a pig's eye! Later, after Bernie talks, the alleged hijackers can dump Cortés safe on the capitol lawn and no one will be the wiser. But maybe we can take advantage of this situation."

"Yeah?"

"Yeah." Brunalesci turned up the collar of his topcoat, putting a finger casually to his lips. A sailor and his girl, holding hands, strolled past them and then stopped, gazing into the window of the Covered Wagon Shop at the Indian jewelry display. The two men walked past them unhurriedly, turned the corner, and kept on around the plaza.

"What if," Brunalesci asked in a low voice, "the media was to get some inside poop about this gang of hijackers, that what they really are is Commie terrorists?"

"Commie?"

"Well, some liberation army, then."

"So?"

"So if some terrorist group is holding the governor, during the rescue some punks could get hurt, like Riley. And like that bastard Bernie. And, of course, with the kind of gunfire you could expect from a bunch of terrorists, the governor might end up with an accidental slug in the brain."

"Jesus! The governor?" Daggett shook his head.

"Think about it. Cortés is driving this drug-traffic crusade. He thinks he can play the game a new way. He's trying to rock the boat, thinks he knows how to swim . . ."

"But the governor!"

"It's been done before—even to presidents!"

Daggett stopped walking, lit his cigar, and looked around for the couple they'd passed. The sailor and his girl were sitting on the steps of the bandstand in the center of the plaza, necking.

"It's up to you," Brunalesci told him. "Just be sure the police search gets delayed until you've located the hijackers' hideout. Then send in Squad B."

The men paused beside the parked Plymouth.

"The governor's death could solve a lot of problems for us, Aldo," Daggett said to Brunalesci.

"Damn right. And if we could get Bernie, Riley, and the governor all at once, we'd be in the clear."

"What about the other hostages, and the rest of the hijackers?"

"Depends," said Brunalesci, "on how much the rest of them see. But I'm sure you can count on Squad B to make certain it's all handled smoothly."

Daggett slid under the wheel of the Plymouth. "Yeah, that's probably the way to go." He started the car. "Got to get back to Santa Fe. I'll keep in touch."

Brunalesci stared after the green Plymouth as it passed San Felipe de Neri Church and turned out of sight. Then he walked rapidly to his own car. He checked the time. He'd better keep New York informed about the situation. That way if Squad B got lucky and shot up the right people in a "rescue" of the governor from "terrorist hijackers," his clients would be happy. But just in case, well, he'd better call. New York might want to fly the pros out to make sure.

SEVEN

After the newscast Rod collected all the hostages' shoes. He was fairly certain none of them would attempt the long hike out of the mountains barefoot in the snow, except maybe Cortés.

Finally, about midmorning, Rod suggested everyone should make a visit to the john before the search began in earnest and they had to stay cooped up.

"Stay close to the big tipi," he ordered. "Right against it. Skirt around the base and slip into the forest. Joe, you stand watch. Miss Morrison, you go with Serefina. I'll take the governor. Cliff, keep an eye on the rest of them until we get back."

Rod unrolled a pack lying next to the tipi flap and extracted two pairs of rubber thongs. He started to hand the largest pair to the governor, but after looking over both hostages' feet, handed the flipflops to Betty Morrison instead. She put them on ungraciously and shuffled out into the snow after Serefina. They heard her swearing as the cold white stuff touched and chilled her bare feet.

Cortés put on his thongs and, supporting himself by his hands on the slanting poles overhead, walked awkwardly to the tipi door, almost stumbling over the others, who sat around the edge, Indian style. Once outside Cortés straightened up, and Rod saw he was limping. In the trees, the men turned slightly away from each other and undid their flies.

Rod said, "You do know we're not going to do you any harm?" No answer. "We had to do this to get some action going, Governor. Otherwise, like everything else, this tax would get debated to death, while big energy continues their campaign to scare us into nuclear power."

"Listen," the governor said, "whether or not you have the right idea, you've done it the wrong way. You *have* done harm, maybe more harm than you know. I have a meeting scheduled at one-thirty that I just can't miss. I'm scheduled to talk with a state witness who will only talk to me."

"I'm sure it's important, Governor—but goddammit, so is this! When are you politicos going to wake up to the fact that you're in the same crummy boat as the rest of us? Quit working for big business, big military, and big government and start working for the people!"

Cortés's black eyes blazed at him. Rod scowled back, his jaw clenched. Suddenly he realized how absurd they must look in the snowy forest arguing politics. Hastily, he buttoned his jeans.

They started back toward the tipi when the governor groaned and sank down slowly. Rod whirled around, ready for an attack, and then saw that Cortés was genuinely in pain. He knelt quickly and examined Cortés's ankle, which was puffy and slightly blue.

"Sprain," Rod volunteered professionally.

"No kidding," the governor replied sarcastically.

Serefina followed Betty Morrison back through the ponderosas toward the tipis. Before they reached the clearing, the lieutenant governor turned to her.

"You seem fairly bright," she began. "Why have you let them drag you into this crazy scheme?" Serefina eyed her silently. "It *is* kidnapping, you know," Betty went on. "You do want to go back to your hubby and kiddies, don't you?" Betty watched her for a minute. Then she added, "Or maybe you'd rather have a job?" Serefina smiled slightly. "Yeah, maybe you'd like a good job—get out of the house, away from the old man—make some pin money of your own?" Betty ran her hand back through her short blonde hair in a confident gesture. "Can you type?"

Serefina answered, "Not very well."

"Well—you could file—yeah, I'm sure you could file." Betty paused. "Look, be a smart girl and help me get out of here. You've got the keys to that bus, haven't you? Help me get away and I'll see you get a nice job at the capitol? You'd like that, wouldn't you?" Serefina stared at Betty Morrison, amazed.

"Haven't you ever wanted a job?" Betty Morrison persisted. "Something you could get good at?" Be proud of?" After more silence, Betty Morrison said, "Being a stenographer at the capitol can be pretty exciting, you know." She gave a sly wink. "Lots of rich guys up there, treat you like a real lady." Serefina wrinkled her brow slightly, as if considering.

"You could say I jumped you, that it wasn't your fault," the lieutenant governor continued. "The rest of them would never know."

Serefina turned and started back toward the tipis, beckoning Betty Morrison to follow. Betty stood for a minute, then stomped angrily after Serefina. She knew she couldn't survive long with no shoes in the snow. "I just wish," she muttered angrily, "more women had my kind of professional ambitions."

"If they did," Serefina said mildly, "the street corners would be awfully crowded." Betty Morrison did a double take. Serefina smiled gently and led her hostage back to camp.

*　*　*

Lauren came back from working in the kitchen tipi to find most of the hostages curled up, dozing. It was still cold in the big tipi, even with the catalytic heater, and it was monotonous. People had crawled into the down sleeping bags Cliff had brought from his bunkhouse supplies.

Senator Claridge was sitting knees up, elbows on knees, hands dangling. Smoke curled from his pipe. He smiled at Lauren as she came into the tipi. It was quiet.

Serefina and her grandmother were preparing lunch. Valencio was standing watch across the clearing in the cover of the trees. Joe, Rod, and Cliff were off scouting. Moira and Ted dozed in the tipi with the rest of the hostages.

Lauren went over and sat beside the senator.

"You look contented," she said after a while.

"Oh, I am," Claridge agreed, drawing on his pipe. "Nothing more fortuitous could have happened to me right now."

"Really?" Lauren was interested.

"Yes." The senator sucked at his pipe and tried to get it going better with his lighter. "I was about to lose my seat after seventeen years—my mistress was threatening to tell all. My wife was hysterical. My constituents were scandalized—ghastly."

He smiled again. "Now, the way things are working out, my wife will be so terrified that something will happen to me, she'll be glad to get me back. And the hijacking—pardon me, protest—will overshadow any other news, so my constituents will be glad I'm back. As for Kathi, well, maybe you could give me some advice." The senator looked sheepish.

"Kathi wants things. Right now, it's just a floor-length ermine coat. But she asks me for things like that because she really wants me to marry her."

"Would you?"

"Oh, my God, no."

"Well . . ."

"Look—Elizabeth—that's Mrs. Claridge—Elizabeth is the only woman for me. I could never marry Kathi. I can't talk to her. She's only twenty-two. I mean—well, we just don't have the same type backgrounds. We couldn't live together . . ."

"Just lay together," Lauren said blandly.

Claridge blushed and pulled at his ear.

"Look, Senator, go home—when you get home—and tell your wife you love her, and that you missed her, and that while you were under duress you realized she was the only one for you. Tell her all you want to do now is have good remaining years together."

"Hmm . . ." murmured Claridge, trying out the idea.

"Then tell Kathi you love her, that while you were under duress, you realized how wonderful she is, but how young, unspoiled, her whole life ahead of her. And that you wouldn't deprive her of the opportunities that might come her way. Tell her . . . tell her . . ." Lauren thought for a moment. "Tell her you love her enough to let her go."

"I don't know if Kathi—"

"Be noble. Be torn. Be brave. Walk away—"

"But I'm not sure that Kathi will believe—"

"Senator, any woman who wants a floor-length ermine coat will believe that . . . *trust* me."

Claridge put down his pipe. "Mrs. Van Dressler," he said, "maybe *you're* the one who should run my reelection campaign."

"Senator," she said, "talk it over with your wife."

He raised an eyebrow, then laughed good-naturedly.

At lunchtime Mercedes had requested an interview alone with the archbishop. Lauren and Moira had padded the floor of the smallest tipi with a tarpaulin and some army blankets. They moved one of the kitchen camp stoves into the tipi and set it up in the center of the floor, which took the chill off the air.

Mercedes led his excellency into the tipi. She settled him, asked him graciously to give her his thongs, put them in her apron pocket, and promised to return at once with his meal.

114

She hurried back to the kitchen tipi to get his lunch. There she found Commissioner Blake sitting beside the Coleman stove, stirring a huge cast-iron frying pan full of hashbrowns and looking as bleak as an abandoned basset hound.

"You are alone?" Mercedes demanded.

He nodded sadly. She saw his feet were bare, but shoes or not, she thought it risky to leave hostages unguarded. Except the archbishop, of course, who would keep his word.

"Eh," she said and began busily preparing a tray for the archbishop with sausages, hashbrowns, tortillas, and a tin cup full of green chile stew. When it was done, she frowned at it. "Oh, the wine," she said aloud. She caught up the tray and, forgetting Blake, hurried to her conference with the archbishop, detouring to the barn where they had hidden the bus. She set her tray on the hood, opened the bus door, and then dug beneath the driver's seat until she came up with a dusty bottle of Bolla Soave. Father Paul liked it; surely his excellency would like it, too.

The archbishop was seated cross-legged on the floor, robe over his knees, rubbing his hands above the Coleman stove. He started to rise as he saw Mercedes enter, but she gestured him down and knelt quickly with the food.

The archbishop eyed her appraisingly. "Thank you for the meal," he said pleasantly. "You are their cook?"

"No, señor," Mercedes said, seating herself. "I am here to speak on behalf of Our Lady of Sorrows Parish. It will take a while, Father," Mercedes told him. "Let us eat."

The archbishop blessed the food, and Mercedes crossed herself fervently. With a plastic fork, Grignard cut hungrily at a sausage that eluded him.

Mercedes began, "Our Lady of Sorrows was built in my village about 1800. The highway it is on was once the King's Highway from Albuquerque to Santa Fe." The archbishop pursued his sausage. "My mother's people built the walls." Mercedes preempted the elusive sausage, wrapped it firmly in a tortilla, and set it in Grignard's hand. "It was a great day for them all when at last they had a chapel of their own, a home for the sacrament, and a place for travelers to hear mass as they traveled the King's Highway."

The archbishop nodded, encouraging her to continue. "Ah, yes," he said, "El Camino Real—like the missions along the coast of California."

"No, señor," Mercedes disagreed gently. "That is California. Here is no El Camino Real—Edeeth Boulevard."

"The King's Highway? Edith?"

"Sí, but our little church building, old as it is, is sound; and it has served the community for almost two hundred years. We were christened there, confirmed there, married there. And there they will say masses for our souls."

"I see," the archbishop said, "a historic monument."

"Oh, no, no, Father—you are still thinking of California. *That* King's Highway. Here everyone has forgotten. There are no monuments on Edeeth Boulevard, just factories and warehouses."

The archbishop looked appalled. "America," he said at last, "I wonder sometimes if you are mighty Babylon, or just the home of the Philistines?"

But this allusion, lost on Mercedes, did not delay the course of the conversation.

"The highway department," Mercedes went on, "decided to make a clover turnaway right where Our Lady sits in the apple orchards."

"Wait, wait, wait," Grignard said, putting up his hands. "What is this clover turnaway?"

Mercedes frowned. She'd never entirely understood it herself. It was something to do with how the cars, all going so fast, passed by and got on and off the freeway without smashing into each other. Suddenly she remembered the wine.

"*Permiso*, Father," she said, rising, and she backed apologetically to the tipi door where her hand found the wine cool from sitting in the snow. She felt in the pocket of her apron,

116

behind the thongs, and produced the corkscrew. "The wine, señor," she said. "I forgot." And she presented the bottle triumphantly.

Grignard read the label. "Señora," he said, "the wine will be an excellent addition." He patted the place beside him where Mercedes had been sitting. "But, as you were telling me . . ."

Mercedes handed him the corkscrew. He started it deftly, turning it as he listened to Mercedes.

"The roof of Our Lady of Sorrows, you see . . . it is new. The beams are hand cut and were put in place by the young men of the parish in 1940. Many of them went to the war and did not come back. We like the beams, you see, because we can see the adze marks of the young men . . . and it makes us feel they are not so far away . . ." Grignard, uncorking the wine, listened, his face intent.

When Lauren peeped out of the tipi to see if there were any signs of lunch, she noticed a slight movement in the shadows of the forest at the edge of the clearing where Valencio was standing watch. Then Lauren saw Rod's red hair and realized the scouts were back.

In a minute Cliff slipped quietly into the big tipi. Everyone stirred as the cold came through the door flap with him. He dropped beside Claridge and Lauren.

"Nothing so far," he said, in answer to their inquiring looks. "Just no sign of any search, which is strange because we're not that far away from Albuquerque. No planes, nothing."

Lauren shook her head. Claridge laughed his big laugh and Lauren put her finger to her lips.

"Sorry," Claridge said, lowering his voice. "I was just thinking. What if we're so insignificant that no one gives a damn we've been kidnapped—and your protest is a bust?" He chortled, amused at himself. "Not that there's a chance in a million that'd happen, but wouldn't it be funny?"

Cliff gave him a dark look. "Hilarious."

"What's going on, do you think?" Lauren asked quietly.

"Don't have the slightest idea."

"News will be on in a couple of minutes. Let's see if there's anything on the radio." Lauren turned the transistor on. The static was bad, but they got a newscast.

In Santa Fe, State Security Chief Hans Daggett says he is investigating several leads to the location and identity of the sunshine tax hijackers who this morning kidnapped the governor and four other hostages at the Hot Air Balloon Fiesta in Albuquerque.

Daggett said preparations are underway for a statewide search. He said he has no plans to call in the FBI or other agencies because the state security force is solely responsible for the governor's safety. In answer to widespread criticism that he didn't immediately deploy search planes in the Sandia Mountains, Daggett said it is essential to the hostages' safety to know how dangerous the hijackers are before troopers move in. He dismissed charges of foot dragging as politically motivated. Earlier today Attorney General Felix Raymond said Daggett was too slow to act and . . .

The static obliterated the news announcer's voice, and Lauren switched off the radio.

"Amazing," Ted said caustically. "Our state security chief is stumbling over himself."

"Teddy, we're on the other side now," Moira said.

"I'm still paying the idiot's salary," Ted snapped.

Cortés said, "Mrs. Findley, I get the feeling you're not entirely committed to this fiasco. And, to tell you the truth, I'm shocked to find people like yourself and your husband involved."

Shrewd, thought Lauren, a direct hit on Moira's social ego. Moira looked mortified.

"I see your point, Guv'nor," Cliff drawled. "It's a frightening thing when your middle class revolts—the ones who have something to lose. It's a lot easier to write off the ungrateful complaining of the ignorant and poor."

"From what I know of rich Texans—and you *smell* like one—this caper is probably your private little safari."

Senator Claridge spoke up. "Governor, I sense a hint of prejudice there. Besides, maybe Mr. Randall's not from Texas? Anyway, what he's said seems to have hit the nail on the head. Hadn't we ought to ask ourselves just what the hell's going on when we're hijacked by a group of fairly reasonable, fairly successful citizens? Does it mean the country's getting sick of the way we're representing them?"

Cliff smiled at Claridge. "Thanks, Senator, for getting to essentials. But Cortés is right. I was born in Rome."

"Italy?" Lauren asked, surprised.

"Texas," Cliff said. "And Texans do have strange ideas. Last summer, when I was in Dallas, I turned my car radio on and heard some self-made millionaire say the government should defend our shores, deliver our mail, fire half the bureaucrats today, the other half tomorrow—and leave us alone."

Ted laughed aloud. "No kidding?"

"'s a fact," Cliff replied. "And I say, long live the spirit of Texas!"

"Then why don't you go back there?" Cortés asked harshly.

"Ah, there's the question." Cliff scratched his temple, which knocked his Stetson back. "Because when I was growing up in Athens . . ."

"Georgia?" interrupted Moira.

"Greece," Cliff said. "I learned to love the light. They have the same quality of light there as we have here in the Land of Enchantment, light from the land of heroes." He smiled. "So when you tax that light, and arouse my distrust of cyclopean government . . . well . . ." He spread his hands and shrugged.

"Gawd, isn't this just too poetic?" Moira scoffed.

"Not really," Ted said coldly. He turned to Cortés. "You know, Governor, I've been sitting here thinking ever since you mentioned you were surprised to see people like me involved. I've known since this started that the charges would be kidnapping. . ." Ted paused. "It's going to be almost impossible to explain—but I'm doing this to fight ugliness."

Everyone listened, curious.

Ted Findley began sweating nervously as he always had in grammar school when he had to recite. But he continued.

"I might have come up with a lot of esthetic dialectic," he said, "but having already made a fool of myself by being here in the first place, I want to say what I mean. Because it's not just the tax . . . but the greed behind it. These things are always justified as expedient.

"First, it'll make solar energy too expensive to be privately used, which is the only economically sensible way to use it; then, nuclear power plants will proliferate. And there will be accidents—pollution—ugliness."

Ted Findley paused, uncertain. He looked uncomfortable, Lauren thought. That had been a tough speech for him to make. Ted had grown accustomed to letting clever remarks serve as conversation.

Moira, obviously embarrassed for him, said tartly, "Ted Findley, boy architect—ta-ta-ta. . ." mimicking a fanfare.

Ted looked at her as if she were a rude stranger.

"Wonderful," Cortés said sarcastically, "a statement of policy."

"That's quite interesting," Claridge said. "And you, my dear?" He smiled at Lauren. "What's your reason for being here?"

"I love a good fight." Lauren smiled back at him.

"That's a little more realistic." Betty's voice came harshly into the conversation. "Rich folks out for thrills."

Lauren turned slowly and fixed her with a cool green stare. Lieutenant Governor Morrison stared back, jaw thrust slightly forward.

"Fine talk. But if you knock out nuclear, you limit means of getting energy to hospitals, factories, food processing plants, schools . . ."

"Nuclear energy's just one way," Claridge put in mildly.

"Listen, Senator," Betty said, "that's great for the ads—

keep the public calm and all—but don't kid yourself. The way fuel shortages are stacking up, this country will come to a screeching halt if nuclear plants aren't built and on line everywhere in five years."

Rod came through the tent flap and let in another breath of icy air. Betty eyed him pugnaciously. "And when everything screeches to a halt," she went on, "there's going to be such misery, such danger, that the very slight possibility of nuclear accident will seem like nothing."

Rod looked at her. "I could hear you from outside," he said. "What you say is true *if* we go on as we are now. But if the nation spends the next five years converting to solar, building mass transit and retooling, there not only won't be a screeching halt—but everyone's standard of living will go up."

"That's idealistic nonsense—"

"Right now it is," Rod snapped, "because of the likes of you . . . and your masters."

Betty jumped up furiously and started toward Rod.

"If you hit him, ma'am," Cliff told her, "I'll slap your hand."

"Sit down, Betty," Cortés said coldly. "Let's not seem more ineffectual than we are." Lauren could hear Lieutenant Governor Morrison's teeth grinding.

Serefina arrived just then with a bundle of steaming tortillas and sausages. She set the heavy Dutch oven in the center of the tipi and passed out foil-wrapped tortillas and styrofoam cups. Lauren wondered if Serefina noticed how quiet everyone had become.

Moira, on the verge of tears, slipped quietly out of the big tipi before lunch was half over. Teddy ignoring her had frightened her more than Teddy being angry at her. He seemed to be pushing her further and further away.

Tears of indignation and frustration stung her eyes. She skirted the big tipi and trekked under the trees to the kitchen tipi where she could be alone. She crept in the doorway, buried her face in her hands, and gave way to piteous sobs.

A soft hand patted her shoulder, and she jumped. Allan

Blake crouched on the floor beside her, like a faithful dog trying to comfort its sad owner. He looked so concerned, she let two more tears slide down her cheeks.

"There, there, it can't be as bad as all that?" he said predictably.

How like him, thought Moira. Much comfort he would be. She cried on.

"Mrs. Findley, what's wrong?"

She turned irritably, but seeing Blake close and concerned, threw her arms around him and buried her head on his shoulder, sobbing hard. He patted her rhythmically.

"It's this whole horrible thing," she choked. "It's like a nightmare. I don't even want to be here. I try hard, I really do, to have a nice orderly life. And one thing or another is always upsetting it. I just want a normal, comfortable life. Is that so terrible?" She hiccuped loudly.

"No, no, it's not so terrible."

At last, knowing her hair was mussed and her nose red, she pulled away and fumbled for a paper towel. She wiped her face and blew her nose. "I'm sorry," she said. "I just always seem to get caught up in things that are happening and having to be a part of them whether I want to or not."

"I know what you mean."

She wiped her face a final time. Thank heavens, it was just Blake. She knew she looked a wreck.

He said helpfully, "There's water in that bucket over there. Why don't you wash your face?"

Moira dampened another paper towel and wiped it over her face. The cold water felt good. When she finished, she asked, "What are you doing here alone?"

"I think everyone forgot about me. That's what usually happens."

"Oh, surely, they didn't," she said politely. They sat for a moment in friendly silence.

"You know what?" He looked shyly at Moira to see if she were listening. She was. He gulped and continued, "When

122

we took off from the field I was so terrified, I thought I'd never get back in one piece."

"I know."

"And you know what I was sorry about?"

Moira shook her head. She noticed Blake gulping.

"I was sorry that I'd given up painting."

She looked at him surprised.

He smiled a little. "That sounds funny, doesn't it? But I always had this wild idea I'd . . . I don't know . . . run away and live in a garret . . . paint, anyway. I was pretty good in college."

Moira was flabbergasted. "You were?" she asked finally.

"I was," Blake insisted, but he sounded uncertain. "I . . . I sold a few paintings before I got started as a CPA. People thought them good enough to buy."

"Then you must have been good. People really bought them?"

"They did. Lovelace Clinic bought two. They used to hang in the lobby. Maybe you've seen them? 'Windmill at Belen' and 'Bosque at Los Lunas'? They're oils."

"I have. Ted and I saw them there. Excellent color. Wait a minute—" her voice grew suspicious—"they're signed—"

"A. Harrell," Blake said. "That's the name I used. My full name's Allan Harrell Blake. I used my middle name, see?"

"Why?"

"Because my parents hated the idea that I might try to make my living by painting."

"But those are *good,*" Moira said. "Teddy even said so. Why did you quit painting?"

Blake shrugged. "Parents—business school—wife—politics—country club—teenagers—everything."

"But as a hobby?"

"No!" Blake said sharply. "I've tried it as a hobby. But painting is not a hobby; it's serious work. I'm a hobby commissioner, a hobby accountant, but I'm serious with oil paints."

"So you're going to paint again!"

"I don't know," Blake said, studying his hands.

"Why not?"

"I'd have to be ready to leave Lindsay."

"Lindsay? Oh, Mrs. Blake?"

The commissioner nodded thoughtfully.

"But surely she—"

"Would you, if it was Teddy?" Blake asked her pointedly. Moira shut her mouth.

"You see?" Blake shrugged.

When Brunalesci was getting ready to leave the courthouse for the day, his beeper went off. He phoned his office and got a message to call State Security Chief Hans Daggett.

"Chief Daggett's office," the girl said briskly.

"This is Mr. Brunalesci, returning the chief's call."

"Just a moment. I'll see if he's in."

"Aldo?" Daggett's gravelly voice inquired.

"Yeah, what have you got?"

"Just a minute. . ." Brunalesci heard the sound of a door shutting. "Aldo? I think we've got a good lead on the hijackers. Some rabbit hunters spotted a bunch of balloons over the mountain north of Placitas. You know, up where they made that movie a couple of years ago?"

"Yeah?"

"They say one of the balloons was silver. That sounds like the solar balloon the governor was in—there's only one solar balloon."

"That's it! That'd be them!"

"I'll instruct the search pilots to report straight to me and no one else if they spot anything. I'll send Squad B up there and make sure all the other units get deployed away from that area."

Thank God, Brunalesci thought as he hung up the phone. Now he had some information for New York.

Tige stood smoking nervously on the escalator as it carried him to the upstairs lobby of the Albuquerque Sunport.

Brunalesci had told him the men from New York would be waiting at the information booth, so it had to be the two in the immaculate dark suits. They didn't appear to be watching for him, though. They stood casually, talking to each other. One wore shades, the other one a hat. They carried topcoats and neither had any luggage.

Tige rubbed his hand nervously over his shiny pate, ran a finger under his collar, and walked over to them. "I'm here to meet you for Mr. Brunalesci."

They looked at him coolly. He waited uncertainly. Both of them seemed to be staring at his neck. He fidgeted with his bolo tie. Their lips curled slightly.

"I've got a car." He jabbed his thumb nervously downstairs toward the front of the building. One of them moved his head slightly in that direction, so Tige led the way.

Outside, Tige climbed behind the wheel of the rented black Lincoln while one got in beside him, the other in the backseat. They maintained a heavy silence. As he swung around the exit, the man in the dark glasses said, "Stop by the Greyhound Station." Brunalesci hadn't said a thing about that, but their silence was so ominous, he drove them down to the station without a word. The man wearing the hat went into package express and returned with a long box stamped perishable. It looked like a heavy waxed florist's carton.

"Now where's Brunalesci?"

"He . . . ah . . . he's waiting for us at Mori's, a bar close to here," Tige said.

"Let's go."

At Mori's, the man in the front seat got out. "I'll be back soon," he said, indicating with a gesture that the other two were to wait for him.

"We could . . . ah . . . walk around the park over there," Tige said after a few minutes had passed.

"We could," the man said, "but we won't."

Tige glanced in the rearview mirror. The man's hat shaded his eyes, but he seemed to be taking an unfavorable inventory of the polyester leisure suit Tige wore.

After another ten minutes, the man with the dark glasses came out of the bar and opened the door on the driver's side. "Okay, I got the location," he said. When Tige didn't move, he leaned over and said, "Bye, bye."

"Brunalesci," Tige began, "says anything I can do to help you . . ."

"Go play!"

"Sure." Tige got out hurriedly. The last thing he saw when the black Lincoln pulled away was the contents of the package as the man in the backseat opened it. It was a disassembled rifle.

Lauren squatted by Rod under the trees opposite the cluster of tipis. The sun had gone down and it was so dusky she could barely make out the conical shapes. Rod was on watch, and she'd brought him his supper.

"You brushed your path with pine boughs coming over here, didn't you?" he asked.

"Yes, everywhere I go, I erase my footprints."

"Good. When the police get their act together and the searchers come around—"

"Why are they so slow?"

"Damned if I know," Rod replied. "Daggett's just not going to rush. Maybe he believes our note and wants to keep the situation from getting out of hand. Who knows?"

Rod took a drink of the hot coffee cautiously. It was laced with rum. "Mmm, perfect."

"That was Cliff's contribution. He stashed a case of Myers in the bus."

"Dat boy do know how to live."

"What does he do, besides ranching?" Lauren asked.

"Getting ready to take him home to mother?" Rod teased.

"My mother," Lauren said distinctly, "comes from *Vermont*."

"Clifford Stallings Randall's mother comes from *Boston*."

Lauren laughed.

"Cliff sits on a lot of boards. But, way back when I met him in college, he told his family—meaning his father—he was going to do it from out here. He bought the Last Frontier and made it go. That's his life. The other's just work he can't get out of."

"Wives? Ex-wives? That sort of thing?"

"Nothing legal," Rod said. "There was a cute thing from Vassar when I met him, but I think it was more his family's idea. She grumbled over the accommodations at the Last Frontier and was gone the next day."

Rod scraped his spoon against the tin cup, picking up the last of the stew.

"You finished?" Lauren asked.

"You settin' your cap for my old buddy?"

"He tempts me."

Before ten o'clock Ted relieved Rod of the outside watch. Rod stumbled tiredly through the trees to avoid making footprints in the clearing. The tipis were barely visible.

At two A.M. Cliff would relieve Ted. Joe would take the next four-hour watch. Rod wouldn't be on again until ten A.M. He could catch some sleep.

The women were standing watches inside the tipi. When he crawled through the door flap, Rod saw by the glow of a tiny penlight pale faces peering out of sleeping bags. Serefina, who had the inside watch, sat by the door, a blanket falling from her shoulders in regal folds. Rod was always surprised by her beauty.

In a hushed voice, Lauren told Rod, "We were about to listen to the news. Maybe they'll say something about the search this time. It's odd that they still haven't started looking for us."

Sitting down heavily on his bedroll, Rod automatically began unlacing his boots. Then he stopped himself. No one was to remove shoes because a barefoot hostage might steal them to escape. He refastened the laces.

Lauren turned on the radio. The newscaster's voice at first made a sputter of static in the drowsy calm of the dark tipi. The static subsided, and the group heard the newscast:

At the top of the news, State Security Chief Hans Daggett announced tonight that the sunshine tax hijackers have been identified as terrorists led by a known heroin smuggler. The chief said the biggest manhunt in the history of the state will begin at dawn tomorrow in the Sandia Mountains for drug smuggler Rodriguez Riley and his accomplices, who are armed and dangerous. Daggett warns citizens to stay out of the mountains and remain on well-traveled highways. Repeat, the state security chief warns the sunshine tax hijackers are terrorists, armed and dangerous . . .

Rod snapped off the radio. Eyes peered at him from strained faces out of shadowed sockets.

"Oh, God," choked Moira.

"That makes us fair game, doesn't it?" Lauren asked in a low voice.

"Yep," Cliff answered. "I'll bet there's open season on terrorists."

"And dope smugglers!" Rod said angrily. "The bastards!"

"But we're not terrorists! Our friends know we're not terrorists! They'll never believe it!" Moira cried.

"People believe what's on the news," Lauren said. "You should know that, Moira,"

"That's right," Serefina said. "You were all ready to believe Rodriguez smuggled heroin. I saw your faces."

Rod looked at Serefina. At that moment he realized he was in love with her. Oh, Riley, he said to himself, you *pendejo*. You're about to go through your clown act again with another woman.

Moira laid face down on her sleeping bag.

"We thought we knew the risk," Cliff said. "But we were naive to assume anyone would believe we're not armed."

"There's more to it than that," Lauren said shakily. "If they didn't believe our note, they'd just say they *suspected* us of

128

being armed. But this business of labeling us terrorists and dope smugglers to discredit us and our motives—that's malicious!"

Betty Morrison said, "You can say malicious? You're the kidnappers! I'm tired of hearing all the bullshit you spout trying to justify your actions. You're outside the law."

Grignard said, "She is right, you know. You are outside the law. And the laws of this nation allow you to protest legally."

Cliff said, "The law's only as good as the people who make it. You, Father, should be familiar with the concept of the letter versus the spirit of the law. Lieutenant Governor Morrison here used the *letter* of the law to pass the sunshine tax."

Cortés said coldly, "You have only one reasonable alternative—release us and turn yourselves in. Otherwise, you risk being killed."

Moira whimpered.

Rod's stomach turned to ice. He felt the desperation of the hunted. The darkness was unbearably close and the fear in the tipi was palpable. He had to get control of himself, think rationally. He had to keep himself from panicking. He had heard that the hunted must fight a growing impulse to surrender. At this moment, all he wanted was to be safe.

In his mind he saw the bullets slicing through his body, Serefina's, Cliff's, tearing away hunks of flesh, spattering brains on the snow. And they'd bleed out their lives as *terrorists* and *heroin dealers*. No one would know otherwise or care. He could feel his hands starting to shake.

He heard Cliff swallow. Lauren stirred tensely. Cortés, lying in his sleeping bag, rolled over abruptly and faced the tipi wall. Then Valencio's voice fell among them like a stone in dark water.

"Many moons ago," Valencio began, "soon—"

Betty Morrison cut in, "This is no time for that Indian crap—"

"Close your mouth, Morrison," Joe said dangerously.

"Many moons ago," Valencio repeated, "soon after the

white brothers stopped killing each other again in the war they called Civil, word came to the pueblos that government schools were to be opened in the white man's state of Pennsylvania. The people were told to make their children ready to receive the white man's education."

Rod noticed Valencio had lowered his calm voice. Everyone, even Betty Morrison, was leaning forward to listen.

"The wise ones sat in council talking of this education," continued Valencio. "Night after night, council fires burned long and low until dawn lit the sky in the east. The white man's train would soon be coming to get the students, for the corn was ripe and melons and fruit were fast becoming sweet. Still no decision had been made, whether to allow the children to be taken to the white man's schools or to make a stand for the Indian way.

"Then Lone Mountain of the Roadrunner People came forth, his blood-red robe drawn around his shoulders. The council was quiet as he began to chant the centuries-old song to our Earth Mother, seeking help and guidance. When the chant was finished, he returned the corn pollen pouch to its spot beneath his robe before he spoke. All listened, for he was well respected.

" 'Have we not passed the teachings of the ancient ones down through the centuries?' Lone Mountain asked. 'Are the teachings not good? We must not let our children be taken from us. Return to your homes before the white man comes and take the young ones up into the canyon. Hide them there in the long-deserted dwellings of the ancient ones. Let them learn the ways of their own people. Teach them to walk in honor as our fathers before. We must not let our children go the way of the buffalo and the seas of grass.'

"The council tasted his words. Then the oldest member of the council spoke. 'Lone Mountain of the Roadrunner People has spoken well, but many remember the Sand Creek Massacre when the bluecoats killed the helpless ones while the warriors were away.'

"The council stirred. Murmuring ran like a wind into the night. The old one spoke again.

" 'If we do as the white man's government wants, our children may be far from us, but they will not be killed.' One by one each member gave a solemn nod. The will of the council was law.

"The day came for the arrival of the trains, and the people of the village made ready to take their children to the railheads. Teams of horses were hitched to the spring wagons. Loaves of bread baked outside in the horno, ears of roasted corn and summer melons were carefully packed in each child's flour sack to sustain him on the long trip.

"Because Lone Mountain was a man of the law, he, too, sent his children. He sent his only son, Gray Cloud, and his daughter, Little Deer.

"Long months passed before the trains returned, and when they did, many of the children were not on them. Lone Mountain's beautiful children never returned. The white man's smallpox claimed both of them before they had been in school three months. Others also had died. Some children chose to remain in the white man's world, already ashamed of their Indianness. The young people who did return came speaking the harsh ugly tongue of the white man. They wore white man's clothes and their long hair, once so proudly worn, was now shorn like sheep at lambing time. They could no longer live in harmony with Earth Mother.

"Many winters later, when Lone Mountain lay dying in his one hundred and eighth year, he said, 'When we let fear rule us, we lost our strength for the future. The fear of the bluecoats took away the seeing of our hearts. We lost everything. The spirits of our children were turned to stone. That day of fear was the beginning of the Indian Nation's fall from glory.' "

In the long silence that followed, Rod slipped out of the tipi.

EIGHT

The night was so dark the stars looked like silver thumb-tacks stuck precisely into stretched black canvas. Rod moved silently into the forest away from the place where Ted stood watch across the clearing. The air had a bite as he breathed it into his lungs. Adrenalin made him move swiftly, and he climbed up the slope strewn with granite slabs that had cracked away from the face of the cliff.

After some time, Rod found himself high above the tipi village on a small outcropping. The valley below was deeply shadowed except for the two grayish spots that were the clearings. The canyon beyond was inky. Rod's fear had run out with the energy that drove him up the mountain. He stood looking past the dark horizon up into the sky. There under black space powdered with distant galaxies, Rod had never felt so alone in his life.

Well, he asked himself, what did you expect? You didn't think they were going to give you a medal for kidnapping the governor, did you?

And a tiny voice inside argued, Yes . . . yes, I thought the good guys would get rewarded.

"Dummy," Rod said aloud and jumped at the sound of his voice. He hunkered down on the windswept granite, looking from the brilliant stars to the dark face of the earth. Whatever was going on, it was clear someone wanted him out of the way. He'd been framed with this heroin story. And evidently someone wanted an excuse to shoot at the rest of them, too, so they'd labeled them all terrorists.

Why do they make up all this crap? he wondered. It's always the same old story. All protesters are dangerous. To hell with how peacefully they protest. Who'll even notice, now, that we're not armed, that we vowed not to hurt anyone? Why did we decide to announce that we had no guns? That was stupid. We set ourselves up for the jackals.

Rod put his face in his hands. Now it was a deadly game. And now he had to be very clear about what he was doing and very clear about who he was fighting . . . and give the rest of them their own choice.

Okay, he thought, start with the idea of giving up. What happens if you give up, take everyone back and tell 'em you didn't really want to play? Game called on account of danger.

Rod took ten deep breaths—his formula for testing an idea. By the time he hit nine his mind was resisting loudly. The guys who took on old King George hadn't backed down when their lives were at stake.

If this protest against the sunshine tax isn't carried through, Rod thought, those vultures at the top will know they can make any kind of decision for us—laws, wars, shortages. That wasn't what the country was set up for.

People had to take responsibility, to be as ornery and independent as those patriots who took on the British Empire. What, Rod wondered, ever made Thomas Jefferson and Company believe a people would fight to keep its freedom? What convinced those guys that people would even notice when they were losing their liberties? Were the signers of the Declaration idealistic fools?

Maybe they were, he decided, but they gave it everything they had when they decided to go for it. Rod stood up and said aloud, "And to this cause I pledge my life, my sacred honor—and what's left of my fortune."

He laughed, and that made him feel better. Okay, Little Chief Big Mouth, he said to himself. Now what about those folks down there in the tipis? Serefina—you gonna let them shoot at her? Cliff? Mercedes? Any of them? *Por Dios*, no!

A thumbnail moon began to rise. Rod knew it was almost two in the morning. He got up stiffly and walked slowly down the hill, stopping occasionally, still deep in thought.

When Ted came back into the tipi after Cliff had relieved him on watch, Serefina asked if he had seen Rod outside, but he had not. Moira took over the inside watch now, so Serefina slipped out.

A thin sliver of a moon was climbing rapidly up the eastern sky. Its dim light barely cut the darkness, making only fuzzy shadows. Serefina walked well away from the tipi, and, in the shelter of a young ponderosa, squatted down. The air was freezing. Just as she finished she heard something stumbling through the trees. It ambled with stops and starts. It sounded like a bear—she knew bear were sometimes seen in the Sandias.

Quickly she stood up, stuffed her shirt into her jeans and tried to zip them. The zipper stuck; she'd zipped the shirt into the fly. Never mind that now. Silently she leaped for a low branch, caught it on the first try, and pulled herself up into the tree. It was a small one, and she couldn't climb high, but she was at least ten feet above the ground, and if she stayed quiet . . .

Serefina clung to the trunk and listened to the rambling progress of the animal. It stopped sometimes, once for so long she thought it had gone in another direction. During that long pause she became aware of the burning cold in her fingers. She had shoved her gloves into the rear pocket of her jeans. Stealthily, she felt for them. There they were. She pulled at them slowly, and as they came free of her pockets she felt the zipper let go of the shirt and her jeans begin to slide down. At the same time she heard the big animal crashing through the seedlings below. She clutched desperately for her falling jeans and lost her balance. She saw the animal large and dark as she fell. Oh, no, it was right below! She was going to land on it . . . *Madre de Dios!*

It grunted loudly as she hit, and thinking it was a bear she began hitting, kicking, and yelling. Suddenly, she was relieved to hear it shouting: "Serefina, it's me! It's me! Cut it out!"

She lay still, panting, and Rod struggled to his knees, clawing the snow out of his face. "I thought you were a bear," she gasped. He pulled her to her feet, and she grabbed for her jeans.

"No, no, it's just me," he murmured, brushing the snow from her hair. He had an arm protectively around her and held her close.

"Rodriguez," she said huskily, "are you going to kiss me?"

He moved closer and put his other arm around her.

"Uh, . . ." she hesitated . . . "before you do . . . would you mind . . . I have to . . . my jeans are unzipped."

"Your what?" he said, startled, letting go of her.

She fastened the zipper and buttoned the top button.

"I was going to the bathroom—" she started.

"In the tree?" he asked, and she broke into wild laughter.

"Never mind," she said when she could talk. "Let's save that story for another time." She tried to see how Rod was taking the whole thing, but it was too dark to see his expression. She was disappointed he didn't try again to kiss her. Well, she thought, that was a real mood breaker. Great way to start a romance. And she almost burst out laughing again.

"Are you ready now?" His voice was amused.

"Ready for what?"

He took her hand and they began walking toward the tipis.

Cortés lay motionless in his sleeping bag, watching the light of day grow brighter in the smoke hole at the top of the tipi.

He puzzled over the hijackers' motives. At first, when he'd

realized he had been kidnapped, he believed the syndicate was behind it. With him missing, the Mafia might be able to flush out Bernie and kill him before he could testify.

But since he had been a hostage, nothing the governor had seen confirmed his suspicions. He'd almost come to believe them when they said the repeal of the sunshine tax was their only motive.

The broadcast last night reactivated his suspicions. Could it be true that the hijackers were actually terrorists and involved in the heroin pipeline as the state troopers said? If so, why weren't they armed? Why hadn't they searched the hostages? He still had his pocketknife.

Could he even believe Daggett anymore? When the frightened Bernie called Cortés to trade state's evidence for his life, he said he'd talk only to the governor. He refused Cortés's offer of state-trooper protection, hinting that the security department was involved in covering up the syndicate's heroin operations.

Cortés wasn't sure what to believe now. The hijackers might be working for the syndicate, they might be terrorists, or they could be what they said they were.

So far, since he'd seen no sign of weapons, he was inclined to believe Riley.

But to take precautions, Cortés had cut strips from the blanket beneath his sleeping bag that could serve as crude footwear. The woolen strips were in his parka pocket along with his pocketknife. If there was an opportunity to escape, he could bind his feet in strips of blanket to protect them long enough to escape out of the mountains.

At first light, Rod went into the kitchen tipi and put on the coffee. When it was perked, he woke everyone in the big tipi.

"You all heard the news yesterday," he said as he poured coffee into styrofoam cups and handed them around. "You know things have changed and that they're very risky right now."

Cliff sat up. Rod watched them all unwrapping themselves from the sleeping bags. It was fairly comfortable in the tipi with heavy clothing and the catalytic heater.

"I gave the broadcast a lot of thought last night," he began. "I'm sure you all did. I decided we ought to talk about it this morning because it could be—not could be, it's going to be—dangerous.

"First of all, I want you to know I am not a heroin smuggler. I've never been involved with drugs in any way. I don't know why the police would say that. I don't know what made them decide we're terrorists, either, but that seems to be the official story and I doubt if it will change. It's an excuse for the law to play as rough as they like, and that means"—he stopped for a long moment—"we could be shot and killed."

No one said anything. "We figured we'd be okay if we made it clear we weren't armed, but it looks like we really were naive. All we did was advertise our helplessness.

"Last night we found out the risk had changed. Before, we were thinking the worst that could happen would be jail sentences. Now it seems our lives may be at stake. I want each of you to realize the danger and decide what you want to do. Those of you who decide to leave can drive the bus into Placitas. It hasn't been identified with us, so you'll be okay."

"That means you're not going, doesn't it?" asked Serefina.

"That's right," Rod said.

"Haven't we made our point? Maybe we should go," Moira said.

"Maybe *you* should, Moira," Rod answered. "Maybe the danger changes things for you."

"I'm not going," Serefina said.

"Look, it's turned into a matter of life and death."

"Oh, come on, Rodriguez," Serefina said. "It was always kidnapping—that's a huge risk."

"Yeah," he admitted, "and I was pretty unrealistic about how it would turn out."

"Maybe we all were," Ted Findley said.

Rod said, "I think so. But given where we are and what's happened—and even what the odds are now—I'm going to stay. Starting and not carrying through is worse than not starting at all. That wouldn't have worked very well in Boston, if all the 'Indians' had gotten scared and run home without dumping any tea."

"Maybe," Cortés interposed, "if you quit this wild scheme now, you'll receive much lighter sentences. But if you idiots hold out until someone gets hurt, you'll get everything the law can dish out."

"Nothing has changed," Valencio announced calmly. "Things have only taken their true form. Was it not this falseness you protested against? Now that it takes off its mask, do not think it is something else."

"That's something to think about," Cliff said. "Did that news bulletin fool all of the people again?"

"Maybe not," Joe said. "People are against the sunshine tax. They'll never believe we're terrorists. It won't work."

"Unless we're killed," Valencio added.

Moira gasped. Lauren said, "Valencio, aren't you afraid?"

He looked at her for a long moment. "Of course," he said.

"Wait a minute!" Cortés said, turning to Lauren and Moira. "No one's going to kill you . . . that's scare tactics."

"Governor," Lauren said, "they're trying to scare us into giving up."

"An important point," Archbishop Grignard said quietly. "However, it is true that things seem to have come to a head, and that danger is very real. I believe Mr. Riley has the right idea—you should all think very carefully what you want, knowing the risks."

An uneasy silence took hold of everyone in the tipi. They stared into their coffee cups, avoiding each other's eyes. Minutes ticked past. Into the silence came the sound of a small plane, loud as a mosquito when you are trying to sleep. It passed high overhead, but everyone knew it was a search plane.

At last, in a quiet voice, Mercedes began gently. "The

138

archbishop now will do all that can be done to save our church, though that will not stop other churches from being destroyed. And why, we have to ask, must it be so?

"It is because everyone goes so fast back and forth, giving himself over to his office and his payments, that no one has time anymore for the apple trees when they bloom. No one builds together the roof . . . no one feasts at harvest . . . no one dances. All the young are busy also going back and forth like ants. That is why they would take down our patient old buildings where the sun comes in different each day as it moves from spring to autumn. No one has time anymore for the way the sun falls, and so it does not matter into what kind of buildings it falls.

"The Good Lord put the sun into the sky and made all that is on the earth for us to care for and enjoy. Surely He wants all His children to be happy in all seasons and not so in a hurry.

"I think I will stay. I am old, but I know everyone must stop running back and forth if the good things are to be left on earth."

"I stay," Ted Findley said.

"You didn't think I'd leave, old buddy?" asked Cliff.

"I'm still in," said Lauren seriously.

Valencio simply gave one sharp nod.

Joe said, "I stay."

They all looked at Moira. "I don't know. . ." she shuddered.

The archbishop spoke up again. "Perhaps it would not be wise to keep Mrs. Findley if she really does not want to be here. I also suggest that Mrs. Sevedra—is it Mercedes?—be taken away from here. I'm sure you can carry out your purpose without exposing those who need not take the risk?"

"Wisely spoken," Senator Claridge said, "as the Swiss have always been wise—and neutral."

"As I recall," drawled Cliff, "their national hero is William Tell."

Grignard chuckled.

Rod said abruptly, "The archbishop is right. We can do

139

what we need to, and most of you can be safe. Serefina can drive Mercedes, Moira, and Lauren back—"

"No!" Serefina said sharply.

"I will not go," Mercedes insisted.

"I'll stay—I'm staying with Teddy—er, Ted," Moira said.

"May I ask," the archbishop held up his hand, "that you take another vote later in the day? Perhaps by then it might seem wise to go."

"I won't change my mind," Serefina said. "I am going to make breakfast." She rose gracefully and left the tipi. Rod followed her outside.

She smiled at him. He loved the way she looked, her lashes thick and dusky, still sleepy, her raven hair tousled so that small wisps curled over her ears. He thought he would say something to tell her how glad he was she wanted to stay, and how desperately he wanted to take her out of danger, but he found himself pulling her to his chest and kissing her hungrily. She kissed him back.

"*Te amo*," he said, "*como te quiero*."

"*Sí, querido*," Serefina replied softly.

During breakfast the plane droned overhead again. Serefina, her lips swollen from Rod's kisses, sat tranquilly beside him. Everyone was inside, all footprints had been brushed out with pine boughs, and Valencio was scouting.

Lauren fixed her own plate last, poured herself coffee, and as she sat down, turned on her transistor radio, keeping the volume low to stifle the rock music. She could hear Betty Morrison murmuring to Senator Claridge and wondered what they were talking about. Cortés ate methodically. Lauren noticed Cliff watching the governor. Good. They should be very careful never to take their eyes off him . . . he was still likely to bolt. And Lauren knew, as she thought the rest of them did, if there was a chance of avoiding gunfire, it would be because the troopers wouldn't want to risk hitting Cortés or the rest of the hostages.

"Oops!" The newscast had begun, and Lauren turned the volume up.

Despite the state security chief's warning that the hijackers are dangerous terrorists, public support of their repeal demand is growing rapidly. In Santa Fe at sunrise more than one hundred demonstrators are marching in front of the round house. They carry signs reading, "Sunshine should be free." Near Albuquerque, citizens are reported flocking to the foothills in attempts to find and join the protesters. Apparently the public isn't buying the official drug / terrorist story and instead is responding to the sunshine tax hijackers' appeal.

"I'll be damned!" said Cliff.
Rod stared with disbelief at the radio, a smile growing on his face. "Shhh!"

State troopers have set up roadblocks to turn back the hijack supporters. However, public response to the hijack is so great that lack of manpower prevents blocking all roads to the Sandias. . . . The Rocky Mountain Telephone Company reports its switchboards in Albuquerque and Santa Fe have been jammed with phone calls from all over the nation urging state legislators to support a repeal of the sunshine tax. An informal survey conducted by this station indicates that most of the hundred and twelve state senators and representatives have decided to support a repeal. All report being besieged by calls. On the lighter side, State Senator Manuel Duran of Albuquerque called this station to report his wife just got out of the hospital with triplets. Duran said, "We need all the sleep we can get. Between phone calls and diapers my life is hell!" He asked the station to inform his constituents to please not call him. "I will support repeal," he said.

A muffled cheer rose in the tipi. Rod quickly gestured everyone to silence. "Let's see how this reaction holds up," he suggested. "If this is what's really going on . . . well, that may change things. Let's wait and see."

The black Lincoln was pulled up hard against one side of the narrow logging road when the ponytailed man in the red Volkswagen saw it. He braked a bit and drove slowly past, going in the opposite direction. The driver's door opened and a man in dark glasses got out. He wore a neat, dark suit. There was another guy in the car, also in a suit, with a hat on. The man on the road put up his hand to halt the Volkswagen.

The girl in the VW beside the longhaired young man put her hand anxiously on his knee. He looked at her quickly, then rolled down his window.

"Say, I'm looking for a place up here, kind of a summer resort thing," the dark-suited man said with a strong Brooklyn accent. "Some kind of Indian village. Can you give me directions?"

"You mean the old movie set?"

"I don't know about movie set—a tourist place."

"It's closed during the winter."

"I want to take a look at it anyway."

"Won't do any good."

"I'm thinking of buying it," the man snapped. "For retirement."

"Okay, mister. Uh, let's see . . . I'm not exactly sure where it is. It's close to here, though. I think—yeah, follow the road you're on. About a mile ahead there's a fork. Turn left—" The young man turned toward the girl and mouthed at her *Keep quiet*, then went on. "Left, isn't it, Sonci?"

She nodded mutely.

"Yeah." He smiled at the sunglasses. "You go through this canyon and it's somewhere on the other side. Maybe two, three miles on."

The man nodded and stepped back. The VW driver waved out the window as he pulled slowly around the Lincoln, then hastily rolled his window up, watching the two men in his rearview mirror as he jounced away in low gear.

"Sonci?"

"Well, it's all I could think of . . . didn't want to use your real name."

142

"But *Sonci?*" she said. "Where did you get that?"

"Made it up."

"I *guess*." She turned around, but the road had twisted through the trees so the Lincoln was no longer visible. "You know they'll get stuck if they get in that mud and ice down in the canyon."

"I know."

"Do you think the sunshine hijackers are at the old movie set?"

"Who knows? It's as good a guess as any."

"Is it back that way?"

"Nope," he said. "It's the way we're going."

"Oh, Carl, do you think we'll find them?"

"They got to be up here in the mountains. No place else they would have gone undiscovered. The state's crawling with cops."

"Do you think anyone else has joined the hijackers yet?"

He shrugged. "Everyone wants to, maybe some have. I dunno."

"I hope we find them. Oh, I wish I'd thought of the hijack! It's great. It's about time. I hope it turns the whole country upside down!"

"It looks like it might," he said, revealing teeth that were the product of expensive teenage orthodontia.

"When my sister called from Seattle, she was so excited! It's an absolute riot up there. She says the whole university's on strike to protest the sunshine tax."

"That's neat."

"Can't you go faster? What if those men turn around? They won't go down the canyon once they see what condition the road's in—"

"Sure they will. They're dumb, you can always spot 'em. They think they're so cool, but you can tell 'em easy."

"Who?" she asked.

"Narcs!"

* * *

143

Cortés lay on his bedroll against the back of the tipi. His watch said it was about a quarter to twelve. The women had gone to prepare the noon meal, except for Betty who was burrowed in her sleeping bag. The archbishop and Allan Blake were dozing, too. Claridge was talking quietly with Cliff.

The governor turned on his side, his back to the others. Carefully he took his knife out of his pocket, and with the two-inch blade scraped at the tough rawhide tipi covering. He had to work slowly not to be noticed, but he'd almost dug a peephole about three inches from the floor. He needed to look out and see if anyone was guarding the bus. He was sure he could hot-wire the bus if he could get to it. Five minutes, maybe ten, if he hadn't lost his touch. It had been over twenty years since he'd hot-wired a car.

He worked at the rawhide where it was thin—slowly, barely moving the blade—until he saw light on the other side of the leather, then more light, and at last there was a small, jagged hole. Cortés snuggled down as if he were sleeping and put his eye against the hole. He was looking at the sheds to the rear of the bus barn.

Cortés slowly rolled his head closer to the wall of the tipi, pulling the bedroll up around his ears so his eye was lined up with the peephole and sheltered from anyone in the tipi. He studied the sheds.

Then he saw hasty movement. Valencio and Joe went into one of the sheds. In a minute they were back outside, trotting away under the ponderosa. "*Qué joda!*" he muttered. Both men were carrying rifles! So, Cortés thought, they *are* terrorists! He tested the thin blade against his thumb. It was still razor sharp. Slowly he inserted the blade in the peephole and began to cut a horizontal slit.

Tonight in the dark, I can worm my way out, he thought, and that'll give me the time I need to hot-wire the bus. Silently he slit the rawhide wall. Then he heard the helicopter. The noise was coming from the direction Joe and

Valencio had taken. Son of a bitch, thought the governor, wonder if I could get to that copter?

The four mounted men rode single file, keeping their horses at a fast, mile-eating trot. They followed a barely discernible logging track through the piñon on the lower slopes of the Sandias. The big man in the lead reined his horse in and dropped back, trotting beside the man following him. All four were dressed in the uniform of the New Mexico state security troopers and wore badges.

"We should be there in about an hour."

"Why the hell did they build this movie set out in the middle of nowhere?"

"Authenticity—no power lines, traffic noise, beer cans, things like that."

"You know that barmaid at La Fonda?"

"The one with the legs?"

"Yeah, her. She was an extra—says they camped up here while the filming was going on."

"How come Daggett thinks the balloon hijackers are out here?"

"Where else could they be?"

"Anyplace. They could be camped out anyplace in the mountains."

"Could be. But I think he's right. It's cold—they'd take whatever shelter they could find. Besides, everyone's pretty much forgotten about the movie set by now. They likely figure it's safe."

"What if Daggett's wrong?"

"Bad news. But chances are he's right. He's got his state boys on every other square foot of ground in these mountains. And nobody's seen any sign of any balloons but those hunters. Right around here."

"You going to radio the chief before we get there?"

"Nope. We'll let him know after we find them."

"After the shoot-out, you mean?"

"Right. After they're dead and we've got the rifles planted on them—after it's all wrapped up nice and neat!"

Both men laughed. "And then," the leader said, "we'll get paid!" He spurred his horse ahead, and single file Squad B continued its steady uphill pace.

It was just before noon and the Forest Service helicopter pilot was hungry. He reached one hand into the paper sack and took a huge bite of the ham sandwich. Mustard seeped from the corners of his mouth and plopped down onto his windbreaker. "Darn!" he muttered to himself as he dabbed at the yellow spots with his handkerchief. Then he wiped his mouth and looked down on the bosomy humps of the foothills. He knew the search for the hijackers was supposed to be widespread over the forested mountainside, but in the whirlybird, with the best aerial view of all, he couldn't see any police activity in the area below him.

He circled the deserted movie set again, leaning over to scan the area on the right side of the chopper. He saw a red Volkswagen chugging along several miles away. From up here the beetle looked like a ladybug. He looked through the binoculars. Flower decals were pasted on the roof. A University of New Mexico sticker was on the back windshield. "Kids," he muttered. "Probably trying to join the protesters."

Now he looked down to his left. He could see a long black Lincoln lurching along a washed-out road. More hijack supporters? If so, they were in for a surprise. The road led only to the muddy bottom of the canyon west of the tipi village. He buzzed low to warn the car to turn back. The Lincoln continued. The pilot buzzed him again. The window on the driver's side lowered. A fist with a fat middle finger extended gestured upward. "Go ahead, you turkeys," the pilot muttered. "It'll serve you right."

A glint of sun on metal caught the pilot's eye. He was right over the canyon now and could see four horsemen, far down the slope, working their way up a path to the canyon rim.

Their silver badges flashed in the sunlight. The men looked up and waved. He waved back.

He flew over the canyon again. He reached down for his thermos and unscrewed the top. Coffee sloshed on his knees. He jumped when the hot fluid hit his skin and dropped the thermos, which rolled on the helicopter's floor. He looked down at the brown puddle, which palpitated with the chopper's vibrations. Below him in the meadow were two figures. One raised an arm and waved to him.

The pilot lowered the chopper and hovered over the meadow a hundred yards from the men. The two stopped, their rifles pointing downward. Hunters, he thought, Indians probably from the Sandia pueblo. They were watching him.

He landed gently in the meadow. The flashing blades reflected light off the barrels of the Indians' rifles. When the blades stopped rotating, the two men approached.

"You two hunting?" the pilot asked.

"Yep," said the old man.

"Rabbits," the younger man said with a grin.

The pilot's eyes narrowed. "Make sure it's rabbits."

The young man glanced at the old man.

"We're staying at the tipi village," the old man said. "We're up here cutting wood, trying to get a rabbit for dinner."

"Seen anybody around here?"

"No," the old man said. "A couple cars. Plenty of planes— scared the rabbits."

"Well," said the pilot, "there's a big manhunt going on."

"We heard about it," the younger man said. "The governor and all."

"Watch out for strangers in these parts," the pilot cautioned.

The Indians nodded.

The pilot waved and lifted off with a roar. Joe and Valencio watched him hop over the tops of the tall pines, then ambled back toward tipi village.

"That must have scared hell outta everybody," Joe ob-

147

served. "They probably thought they'd have a chopper in the tipi with them."

Valencio led the way swiftly through the forest. When they arrived at the tipi village he stayed under the cover of the trees, circling the clearing and listening.

Inside the big tipi everyone was silent, listening for the buzz of the helicopter. They couldn't hear it now. Had it landed? Rod wondered. He looked at his watch—noon! He snapped on the transistor to hear the news, keeping the volume low.

Not since the Double Eagle II crossed the Atlantic have balloons so captured the nation's imagination. Sunshine tax demonstrations are being held today throughout the country. In Boston, citizens dumped thousands of tea bags labeled *Sunshine Tax* into the harbor, site of the Boston Tea Party, America's original tax revolt more than two hundred years ago.

And in the nation's capital, the president said he would make no comment on the hijack or the sunshine tax until the governor and other dignitaries are released. While the president held his news conference, hundreds of pickets carrying "Down with the Sunshine Tax" placards marched in front of the White House.

In California, birthplace of Proposition 13, demonstrations against the sunshine tax are being held up and down the coast. An estimated five hundred demonstrators paraded in downtown San Francisco with signs reading, "Gays like suntans, too." In Los Angeles, several thousand young people converged on the beach carrying surfboards painted with the slogan "Sunshine Should Be Free."

And in New Mexico, site of the hijacking, despite Security Chief Hans Daggett's warning, citizens by the hundreds have gone into the rugged Sandia Mountains where the hijackers are believed to be holding Governor Cortés and the other hostages. . . . Milton Mossberg, a physicist at Los Alamos Scientific Labs, who was apprehended trying to run a roadblock in a snowmobile, explained to Channel 7 why he did it.

"I make my living developing nuclear power," he said, "but I defend to the death everyone's right to the sun."

* * *

When Rod heard the whir of the chopper, he cut off the radio. The helicopter made two more passes over the tipi village. At the door, Rod peered up at it through a crack. He was afraid it was going to land. Then he saw Valencio under the trees on the far side of the clearing. Valencio kept on walking, as if he couldn't hear the chopper. "*Cabrón!*" Joe followed him.

"Oh, no!" Rod groaned.

"What?" Cliff whispered.

Rod made room for Cliff to look out. Valencio walked slowly out into the center of the clearing, Joe trailing him, and waved upward. The copter flew low overhead and buzzed away south. "Son of a bitch!" said Cliff.

Rod moved back from the door, aware of the bodies pressed close behind him and a cold wind on his feet. Turning, he saw the slit close to the floor of the tipi.

"Jesus Christ!" he said. "Governor Cortés has escaped!"

NINE

Rod could hear Serefina scrambling on the slope below him as he worked his way along the rim of the canyon. Granite boulders that had broken away from the rimrock lay in tumbled heaps from the lip of the canyon to the creek bed two hundred feet below. It was rough going down there, climbing over the fallen rock and scrub oak. Up here, the forest floor, carpeted with pine needles, stretched out smoothly between the giant ponderosa. The snow had melted in places where the sun reached it during the day. If Cortés were up here, he'd have to be chased and tackled. Rod prowled along searching systematically among the red-barked trunks for Cortés's bright yellow parka.

Suddenly, he heard Serefina call, her voice echoing up and down the canyon. "Governor Cortés—stop!" There was an answering shout from Cliff a little way up the canyon, then the sounds of several people scrambling through the rocks on the slope below.

Rod ran to the rim of the canyon and, easing himself between two large boulders, looked down. The governor was directly below him, about twenty feet downslope. Serefina and Cliff were moving toward Cortés from either side. The governor was blocked from the bottom of the canyon by a ridge of huge fallen stone and deadfall timber that had accumulated against it. Rod saw Cortés eyeing the talus slope upward. He hasn't seen me yet, Rod thought, and if he makes a run for it, it'll have to be in my direction.

A movement on the opposite rim of the canyon caught Rod's eye. He looked up, startled to see the shape of a horse and rider dark against the sky. The man pulled in his roan, looking down over the canyon, and Rod saw it was a state trooper. "Goddamn," Rod swore, "the cookie has crumbled." The cop had spotted the governor's bright yellow parka, no doubt about it. Rod saw him direct a pair of binoculars toward Cliff, Serefina, and the governor. Not one of them had yet seen the horseman across the canyon.

Then Rod saw the cop lift a rifle to his shoulder and sight in on the group below him through his scope. "Hey," Rod shouted, jumping up, "hey, don't shoot—that's the governor!" The cop jerked his head up but couldn't locate Rod between the granite boulders. In a second, Cortés spotted Rod and followed his stare across the canyon to the mounted state trooper.

The governor waved and shouted, "It's me, Governor Cortés—over here!" Rod watched incredulously as the cop swung his rifle back at Cortés and took careful aim. "*Cuídate!* Watch out! He's going to kill you!" Rod yelled.

The governor's head snapped around at the Spanish command, and Cortés stumbled on his uneven footing and fell forward, an instant before a shot exploded through the gorge.

Rod started moving toward the governor at the same time Cliff and Serefina closed in on him. "Get down!" Rod shouted desperately. "Stay away from the governor. That guy's shooting at *him!*"

It was no use. All three of them clustered together below him as he saw the horseman take aim again. Rod started down the slope in gigantic leaps and threw himself into a horizontal block with everything he had, hitting the three below the knees. The impact of their bodies and the second shot came simultaneously. They rolled down the slope and slammed against the boulders at the foot of it, almost halfway down the canyon.

Rod spit dirt and dove across the governor, pinning him down. "They're shooting at *you*, Cortés," he gasped. "Stay down, we've got some cover here."

"Umph!" the governor grunted, "get offa me!" Rod rolled aside hastily and scrambled up closer to the big rocks. Serefina was flat on the ground in front of him, her head close to his. Her eyes were so large and dark in her pale face, she looked like a small nocturnal animal flushed into the daylight and stunned by it.

"Cliff," Rod rasped. He lay face down behind Rod. Cliff made a muffled sound.

"We've gotta get the hell outta here," Rod said.

Cliff groaned. Rod crawled up to his friend and turned him over. A red stain was spreading across the front of his sheepskin jacket from the right shoulder. *"Hijo madre,"* Rod swore.

"Hurts like hell," Cliff grimaced, "so don't ask." Serefina crawled up beside Rod. She gasped when she saw the red-stained coat. "We've got to stop that bleeding," she whispered.

Cortés had edged away from them some distance to the end of the rock pile, but now began inching back. "The cop's got a field radio," he told Rod. "He's talking to someone. He's riding along the rim now, looking for a way down."

"Damn," Rod growled. "We'll have to move fast. It'll take that son of a bitch maybe fifteen minutes to get his horse down through those rocks and up here. That's how long we've got. So level with me, Cortés, what the hell's going on? They're shooting at you!"

"But maybe they're shooting at you, too?"

"Goddammit, yes, we're supposed to be terrorists—but why you?"

"Because," Cortés said through his teeth, "I'm about to

152

put some people out of business—the narcotics business." He looked Rod in the eye.

"Governor," Rod said, "I don't know what in hell you're talking about."

"Maybe," Cortés said, and for the first time he smiled.

Looking at Cortés's proud Hispanic face, Rod really liked his fierce young governor. The guy was okay. He wasn't scared, just mad. And he was cool headed.

"Okay, let's get you out of here," Rod said. "Take off that damn yellow parka."

Cortés peeled it off and thrust it under a rock. "Here, put this on," Rod ordered, struggling out of the shapeless brown coat he'd worn during the hijacking. "It's camouflage. There's a stocking cap and sunglasses in the pocket. Put them on, too!" Cortés obeyed.

"It might work," Rod said, "if they're gunning for you and not me."

"Listen," Cortés said, "whoever gets shot, they'll wipe out the witnesses." Rod knew Cortés was right. These weren't cops rounding up demonstrators. These guys meant to kill.

"Try to edge over to that ridge of rock with the big fallen tree across it," Rod said. "I think you can stay covered behind the trunk and work your way to the top. Then you'll have to run across the open slope into the boulders at the rim of the canyon. Get back to camp. Mercedes has the keys to the bus. Take everyone who's there and go. East of here you'll pick up Highway 14 to Santa Fe."

"What about you?" Cortés asked.

"I've got to take care of my compadre," Rod said. "That'll slow us down some."

Cortés grasped Rod's hand. "If I make it, amigo, you'll get help pronto. *Vaya con Dios*." He crawled away, hugging the boulders they were hiding behind.

Rod turned to go back to Cliff and drew in his breath. Serefina knelt by Cliff, her lovely slim back naked, ebony hair falling across smooth ivory skin. As he watched, she quickly pulled on her jacket and fastened it. Rod saw she was using her flannel shirt to pack Cliff's wound. Rod worked his way toward them.

"Bad bleeding," Serefina told him. She pulled Cliff's blood-stained jacket around his chest and buttoned it firmly. He was pale, and perspiration had broken out on his face.

"Cliff," Rod said, "can you walk?"

"Sure," Cliff answered, "probably run, too, if they shoot at me."

"*Bueno.*" Rod touched his hand. "Then let's figure how to get out of here." Rod smoothed Serefina's hair gently away from her forehead, then edged between the jumbled slabs of granite and inched forward on his belly until he could see down into the canyon.

The horseman who'd shot at them was about a third of the way down the opposite side of the canyon, working his horse back and forth among the boulders, picking his way downhill. Then Rod saw there were two more mounted men on the canyon rim above the cop, and as he watched, a third horseman joined them. They all three pulled rifles out of their saddle scabbards, and carrying them in one hand, followed the leader in his slow zigzag descent to the canyon bottom.

Rod squirmed backward to Cliff and Serefina. Cliff was on his knees now, not looking any better. "That way?" he asked, nodding at the rock and timber deadfall along which Rod had directed Governor Cortés.

Rod scanned the canyon side. Cliff was right. It was the only way that would offer any cover until they were close to the top. They would have to run up a short open slope to the rim where the fractured rock would shelter them. And that's about Cliff's limit, Rod thought.

A shot broke the stillness and roared up and down the canyon in deadly echoes, followed by a second and then a third shot. Rod looked to the top of the rocky ridge and saw Cortés fall back behind it. Had he been hit? No, he was on his knees, crawling in closer to the huge fallen tree. Goddammit, they'd spotted him, and now he couldn't make his escape across that open ground.

Suddenly six or seven shots in rapid succession rang out over their heads from the rimrock above them. They were surrounded! Someone was behind them up on the canyon rim!

"Serefina, get Cliff up there with Cortés," Rod said in a low voice. "I'm going after those bastards on the top." Rod started edging over to where he figured he could make his run for the top. If he was right below the gunmen, he might make it before they saw him.

He heard more shots from the horsemen on the opposite side of the canyon. He saw dirt and splinters spray off the rimrock above him. Holy Mother of God—who was that up there? The cops were shooting at them, too!

Blood-chilling screams ripped through the canyon, magnified and reverberating. Shots from above—more screams. The place sounded like Indians attacking a wagon train. Indians! Rod saw Valencio pop up to wave a rifle at him and duck back behind the rimrock. The firing continued. Hot chachoolies, the Indians had guns! Rod laughed aloud. Now where in hell did those guns come from?

He stuck his head cautiously over the rocks. The riders on the other side of the canyon had taken cover and were still firing at the Indians. Rod scrambled back to Serefina and Cliff.

"Let's go," he yelled over the gunfire. "That's Valencio and Joe covering us with rifles."

Cliff smiled slowly. "Well, I'll be damned—a cavalry rescue."

"Yeah, old buddy." Rod laughed. "Let's mosey on back to the fort."

Serefina led the way, Cliff dragged himself after her, Rod right behind him. The firing continued from both sides of the canyon as they worked their way up the deadfall where Cortés was crouching.

The governor's mirrored lenses reflected their grins as they approached him. "Who the hell is that?" The governor gestured at the canyon rim above.

"It's okay, Governor, that's Joe and Valencio—and they're still on our side."

The firing from above continued furiously, answered only sporadically by the cops, who were taking careful aim. Rod realized they'd lost the element of surprise. The troopers would pick them off as they ran across the talus slope. Rod studied the distance, trying to figure out how to get them all safely to the top.

Beside him, Cliff lay face down, breathing heavily. Rod looked at him, and then back at the slope. "Riley, look at that rock over there," he heard Cliff say.

"Where?"

"Put your head down here. You can see it from underneath this log."

Rod looked under the fallen pine. He saw instantly what Cliff meant. A huge slab of granite was balanced precariously on the ridge they were hiding behind. If it could be pushed free, it would start a landslide down the canyon and maybe provide the diversion they needed to make their break.

"Come on, Governor," Rod said, "we're going to start a landslide." Cortés followed him as he bellied his way under the fallen tree. Without a word, they put their backs against the trunk and pushed the boulder with their feet. Serefina was holding Cliff's arm, and Rod saw they were tensed to run. She looked at him once, black eyes enormous. Rod doubled his efforts, and the slab slid slowly off the ridge. It turned over ponderously. They could hear it picking up other boulders and the smaller stones bouncing ahead of the slide. Dust boiled up as Rod and Cortés hurried back to Cliff and Serefina.

Rod grabbed Cliff and shoved Serefina ahead of him. "Run!" he commanded. The governor gripped Serefina's arm and the four of them burst out from behind the deadfall as the landslide rumbled down the canyon, punctuated by the sharp crack and whine of echoing shots.

Rod heaved Cliff over the rimrock, and all four crouched behind it, gasping for air. They had made the top! They were safe for the moment. Cliff's color was terrible, but he looked determined. Serefina's shirt seemed to have stanched his bleeding.

"Come on," Cortés muttered, hauling Cliff to his feet. Cliff leaned on Cortés, and they started in the direction of the tipi village.

"Load everyone in the bus," Rod told Serefina. "Get to a phone as fast as you can!" Then Rod took her in his arms and kissed her. "*Hasta la vista.*" She turned and ran after Cliff and the governor.

Rod ran up canyon, keeping back from the edge. The shooting continued, but it had slowed down. It sounded now as if Joe and Valencio were simply exchanging shots with the cops on the other side of the canyon.

When Rod looked back, the governor, Serefina, and Cliff were out of sight. Up ahead he saw Valencio. Double bandoliers were crossed over his chest. On the ground beside him were three more filled with cartridges. The old man looked up casually from where he squatted behind the rock.

"Give me that rifle," Rod said. "I'm going to kill those *putos!*

Valencio calmly shook his head and fired another round. "No ammunition," he said matter-of-factly.

"Then what the hell are you firing?" Rod asked, pointing to the bandoliers.

"Blanks."

"*Blanks!* You're shooting blanks?"

"Movie guns," Valencio said, firing three more rounds quickly. "From tipi village. Cops working down hillside. We better go before they catch on."

"Oh, Jesus. Okay, chief, let's go!"

Valencio threw back his head and howled like a wolf, an

eerie, menacing sound that carried down the canyon. Rod heard a few more shots, then the eerie howl was answered from farther along the rim, where Joe was.

"What's it mean, that howl?" Rod asked.

The old man looked at him gravely. "It means save your ass."

Rod and Valencio trotted through the trees toward the tipi village. As they neared camp, Joe came out of the forest toward them carrying a prop rifle.

"Cops not moving," Joe panted. "Wolf cry makes them cautious."

"Wolf cry maybe buys us five extra minutes," Valencio said, not breathing heavily at all.

The bus was still in the shed, but Serefina had it running. The engine chugged uncertainly, warming up. The rear doors were open, and Rod could see everyone was inside, squeezed in among the bulkily packed balloons. Rod leaped into the bus and pushed his way to the front.

"Don't bother backing out and turning around," he told Serefina. "We haven't got time. Drive right through the wall. It's half rotted away and'll come down like cardboard."

Serefina nodded, her attention on the sound of the ancient motor, which was beginning to fire more evenly. She put the parish bus in gear and backed out of the shed, gunning the motor for her forward run.

Rod looked around at the silent passengers. Whatever Serefina and the governor had told them, they seemed to realize they were all in danger. Faces were tense.

Cliff was lying half conscious on one of the seats at the front of the bus, held in Lauren's arms, her breasts cushioning his head.

Moira Findley knelt on the floor beside them, bandaging Cliff's shoulder. Her thin face was dirty, her hair straight and pushed back like a young boy's. Her makeup had worn away hours ago. Why, she's a pretty woman, Rod thought.

Moira taped the bandage, closed the bus's first-aid kit, and looked up at Rod. "The bullet went straight through," she said. "Right above the collar bone. I've cleaned it the best I could and packed it to keep the bleeding down." The revving engine drowned out her voice.

"Wait!" Senator Claridge yelled. "The Indians!"

Rod looked back. Valencio and Joe were running toward the bus from the storage shed. Joe, with several rifles under each arm, had a coil of rope and half a dozen cartridge belts draped over one shoulder. Valencio carried a wooden box in his arms. They leaped through the rear opening as Serefina gunned the bus forward. The long old hood hit the flimsy plank wall and it splintered apart as the bus burst out of the shed and started along the dirt ruts toward the back road to Santa Fe.

"Get up here and give Serefina directions!" Rod yelled at Valencio. "What took you so long?"

Valencio dropped the wooden box. As it thudded on the floor of the bus, the lid flew off and several cartridges bounced out and rolled across the floor.

"Souvenirs," Valencio said.

Rod shrugged apologetically. Valencio was like some of the old sheepherders Rod had known when he was growing up. Quiet, gentle men who went about their work patiently, never missing any detail, men who, if provoked, would slit throats with the same efficient calm.

Cortés stared at the rifles and ammunition, astonished.

"Easy, Governor," Rod said. "These are movie guns— props. The cartridges, sad to say, are all blanks."

"You mean you rescued us with *blanks*?" Cortés asked Valencio.

Rod handed Cortés a rifle and a cartridge belt. Cortés examined them.

"Well," the governor said, "maybe they'll come in useful again." He slipped the bandolier over his head on one side and the rifle strap over the other.

Stripes of shadows from the tall pines flickered across the bus as it rattled along the logging road. Joe stationed himself at the window with his rifle. There was no sign of the mounted troopers.

Valencio stood behind Serefina, directing her right or left as they approached forks in the road. Mercedes sat beside a window praying steadily in Spanish, holding her rosary. Allan Blake inched up beside Rod, his pudgy face pale. "What's she saying?" he asked nervously.

"She's praying for Cliff," Rod told him, "and that the bus will get us to safety."

Hans Daggett left Santa Fe driving south just fifteen minutes after he had received the relayed message from Squad B. One of the state units had intercepted the coded radio call and phoned it in. The quarry had been sighted. His coded reply was brief: "I'm on my way."

He got behind the wheel and drove out on Highway 14, bearing down on the gas pedal. The radio blared. Helicopters and cars were continuing their search west and south of where he now knew the governor and his kidnappers had been located. Instructions had been given for the roadblocks to be maintained. He pulled a Muriel from his pocket, bit off the tip, spat it out, and lit up cheerfully. Squad B should have the governor and the hijackers trapped by now. Daggett was confident he could stop the drug investigation. He and his boys should have another profitable ten years.

"We should come to Highway 14 any time now," Valencio said to Serefina. "It will be smoother on the pavement."

Lauren held Cliff, who was drowsing. As the bus lurched along, he'd wake up from time to time, mumble apologies, and drift off again. "Shhh," Lauren crooned, "sleep, just sleep."

Moira said worriedly, "I think he's in shock. I wish I knew more. I haven't worked as a nurse's aide since I was in college, years ago."

She stared at her iodine-stained fingers. Then she looked up at her husband. He smiled at her. She went to him, and he held her quietly. "Oh, Teddy, I love you," she said. "I've been such a ninny. We were going to do so much together. You were going to build as you'd always dreamed you could. We were going to"—she gave a little sob and choked out— "live."

Ted patted her gently. "Moira, Moira," he said softly. But tears had begun running down her face.

"Oh, Ted, we should have gone to Tunis when you had the chance to build that compound. I'm sorry, I shouldn't have fought against it. Instead, I made you take that shopping center in Phoenix."

"It was a huge commission," Ted reminded her. "It really got great publicity."

"Oh," Moira cried, "but that wasn't what you wanted. And children—we should have adopted, like you said."

Ted lifted her up and sat her on a balloon packed in one of the gondolas. He handed her his handkerchief and she wiped her eyes and blew her nose.

"Time's gone by so fast," she murmured, "and it's too late to get any of it back—it's too late."

"Don't be a goose," Ted told her. "I love you. It's not at all too late for anything."

Rod thought Serefina drove the bus as if she were piloting a plane, every sense alert, giving it just the right speed on the curves, pushing it along as fast as it would take the road. They'd been on the paved highway for several minutes, and now Rod was sure they could outrun the horsemen with no trouble.

Inside the bus, everyone was so quiet Mercedes's murmuring could be heard as she finished the Lord's Prayer—"and deliver us from evil . . ."

"For Thine is the kingdom and the power and the glory forever. Amen," Senator Claridge finished up. Then he turned to the governor. "Juan, what is going on? If my life is on the line, I want to know."

Everyone turned toward Cortés. "I'm not exactly sure myself," Cortés began, "but here's what I *think* is going on." He spoke earnestly, his face intense. "Some *pendejos* are trying to suppress the government of this state."

Archbishop Grignard seemed to be trying not to smile. In a moment, Rod realized the reason. Cortés was half sitting on a packed gondola, one fist on his hip, festooned with cartridge belt and rifle. His jaw black with stubble, his feet swaddled in "Valley Forge boots," he looked like a classic revolutionary.

"When I said I was going to bust the narcotics traffic through this state, way back during my campaign, I should have known the dealers couldn't have run their operations without payola somewhere in the security force."

"But you know this now?"

"Yes. By luck there's a witness, a Bernie Martinez, state security chief's special lieutenant. He claims he was involved in the syndicate drug operation and then got in trouble with the Mafia for moonlighting on the side. The Mafia's after him, and he's offering to be a witness—to name names—for my word that I'll provide protection for him."

"Your word?" Rod asked.

"I *am* the governor," Cortés reminded him.

"But, what I mean is, why doesn't he just tell Daggett?"

"Maybe he figures Daggett can't offer the special protection I can arrange with the feds—a new identity, a new life. Or maybe Bernie has reason not to trust Daggett. Anyway, he'll talk to me and to no one else. I was supposed to meet Bernie and the attorney general yesterday right after the balloon festival."

"And then we hijacked you."

"Yes. I was sure there must have been a leak and the hijacking was to keep me away from that meeting and give the syndicate time to find Bernie and kill him. Without him, there's not much chance to crack this operation."

"Where's Bernie now?"

"I don't know. He was going to stay hidden until our meeting. So suspicious he wouldn't accept state trooper protection until he talked with me."

"But the troopers were trying to kill you, Governor."

Suddenly the bus coughed and lurched, then coughed again. The engine stopped, and they were coasting along the road trailing a cloud of blue smoke.

"My God, what now?" Betty Morrison cried, jumping to her feet.

"What's the matter, Serefina?" Rod asked quietly.

Serefina's voice trembled slightly. "I think we're out of gas. The gauge reads empty."

"But no," Mercedes insisted, "it cannot be! I filled it full in Alameda before we left for the balloon fiesta. We should have miles left!"

"We should," Serefina agreed, trying again to start the motor as they rolled downhill, "but the gauge registers empty."

"Try again," Rod urged, but the bus was slowing as the grade changed, and they rolled uphill, losing momentum. No one spoke as Serefina steered the bus onto the shoulder of the highway and it came gradually to a halt.

"Everyone stay in the bus," Rod ordered. "I'll find out what the trouble is. If it's bad, we'll have to . . ." He left his sentence unfinished and he jumped to the ground after Serefina.

As soon as they reached the back of the bus, they spotted the trouble. Gasoline still dripped from the punctured tank.

"We must have torn it coming through the shed wall," Serefina said. "Look at that gash in the metal."

Rod wiped a hand across his mouth. He had fourteen people to get to safety, and it was a sure thing they weren't going by bus.

Miles behind the bus, Squad B loped along Highway 14. All four horses were lathered up and their sweaty flanks gleamed in the late afternoon sun. The horses had not rested

163

since the pause that followed the last wolf howls. When no further shots were fired, the riders had radioed Daggett before working their way to the canyon bottom. Then they risked riding openly up the slope from which the shots had come. At the rock pile, one of the men called out, "Hit someone, and pretty bad to look at the blood."

Their quick search of the deserted tipi village uncovered prop rifles and boxes of blanks.

"Well, I'll be a son of a bitch," the squad leader said. "They're fighting us with popguns!" Smiling like a jackal, he mounted his roan gelding and led his men on a fast trot along the tracks in the snow, which showed clearly every turn the bus had taken down the logging road.

The chief was on his way from Santa Fe. They all knew how big the cash bonuses would be if they were able to kill the governor, that redhead, and Bernie, who was sure to be with them. But even if Daggett reached the hijackers first, Squad B would be well paid to be in at the kill. The leader dug his heels into the roan.

TEN

Rod opened the back of the bus and yanked out the first gondola. "This is as far as the bus is going," he informed everyone. "We've got a chance in a million to get away before those riders catch up with us. There's only one way for us to go—up!"

The others moved quickly to unload the baskets. The commissioner jumped heavily to the ground and held up his arms for the gondola Joe heaved from the back door of the bus. He staggered under its unexpected weight, and Rod helped him lift it down.

"Ted," Rod yelled, "take the fan and get this balloon up. Senator, give him a hand. He'll tell you what to do."

As Ted struggled to get the *Rainbow's End* inflated, the other four balloons were unpacked and rolled out in a line on the blacktop. They lay there like huge, rumpled throw rugs, their colors and patterns running into each other insanely.

"We have only one fan," Rod said, "so we'll have to take turns. Flap your balloons to get as much air into them as you can while you're waiting."

Rod strained his ears for galloping horses over the whoosh and snap of the voluminous material and the whirring of the fan.

Ted hefted the big fan away from *Rainbow's End*. "You can have this now," he shouted. Valencio grabbed it, and he and Joe positioned it at the *Windfoal*, which quickly began to fill as the fan blew in cold mountain air. Out of the corner of his eye, Rod saw the governor helping Serefina flap air into the *Sun Power*.

Cortés goes in the first balloon, Rod decided, with Cliff and—Lauren. Lauren was going to get to fly a balloon, after all. Thank God we still have a pilot for each balloon, he thought, even without Cliff.

"Rod!" Moira called in a worried voice, "something's wrong with the *Artful Dodger*. Nothing's happening!"

Rod rushed over and began inspecting the nylon.

"Aw, hell!" he groaned. "The deflation panel must have been ripped off when Joe and Valencio hit the outhouse. We'll have to manage without the *Dodger*. Don't waste time on it. You and Betty inflate the *Camelot*."

We're short one balloon, he thought, and he started counting. Fourteen people. Four balloons. Three to a balloon. Three times four is twelve. The number seemed to flash before his eyes: Twelve, twelve, twelve. Two people would have to be left behind.

Who should I keep with me, he wondered, watching them as they worked frantically to get the balloons inflated. Of course, it couldn't be one of the pilots; they were needed to fly the balloons. And who would have the stamina to survive what might lie ahead? He glanced at each one, his eyes settling on Valencio. Yeah, Valencio was a tough old bird.

He ran back to the bus where he found Cliff half out of it. "Sorry," Cliff mumbled. "Not much good . . ."

"Be quiet, amigo," Rod replied. "I'm going to put you in *Rainbow's End* along with the governor. Lauren will be your pilot. Hang on now." He slung Cliff's good arm over his shoulder, and they walked slowly together along the highway's edge where the snow had melted. Rod lifted Cliff over the railing of the gondola. Lauren squeezed Rod's hand.

"Cortés!" Rod bellowed. "Get your ass over here! You go in this one. Get in!"

"No. I'm not going."

"The hell you say!"

Cortés put up his hand. "I know, I know, but you're assuming that once we're airborne we're automatically safe."

Rod stared at him.

"Can't you see, *hombre?* By being in a balloon I'd put all your people in jeopardy." The governor shook his head. "We know they have long range rifles. If they're shooting at me, they could hit anyone." He glanced down at Cliff, slumped on the floor of the *Rainbow's End*.

"You have a point," Rod admitted. He chewed his lip. They'd have just seconds after the first sound of galloping hoofs, then the killers would spot them. Those in the balloons would have to get up fast. Those on the ground would have to run like hell. He needed someone who could sprint.

He looked at the governor. Cortés was cool, fast, and fit. It hadn't been so easy to catch him back there in the meadow where the *Camelot* had crashed into the pines.

"Okay," he said, "there's only room in the balloons for twelve people, anyway, so you and I will take our chances together on the ground.

"Get in the balloon, Betty," Rod ordered. The governor helped the lieutenant governor into the swaying *Rainbow's End*.

Rod had already turned to Lauren. "Hold close to the ground if you can, until the others are airborne," he instructed her. "Then blast her—pop up—but not too soon, or you'll give away our position."

"How bad do you think Cliff is, Rod?"

"We've got to get him some help pretty fast." He kissed her cheek and let go of the basket. "Give her some gas. Okay, blast again. Okay!" He heard Cliff groan as the *Rainbow's End* bumped along the blacktop and rose giddily into the air.

"The *Camelot's* ready, Rod!" Moira called.

Rod hurried over. Moira was in the basket testing the torch like an old pro. The senator and Allan Blake were watching her uncertainly. The white balloon seemed impatient to be off, responding to a slight gust of wind.

"Get in," Rod ordered the two men abruptly. "Moira, try to stay down close to the other balloons if you can. Okay, lift off!"

Two more balloons to go. Rod looked at his watch. Time counted heavily against them now.

"Hurry up, you guys!" he called impatiently to Joe and Valencio. They were still using the fan on the *Windfoal*, which was about half inflated. "Get that fan to Serefina fast! There isn't a minute to spare!"

Ted and Serefina were still flapping the *Sun Power*, but she wasn't responding as well as the other balloons had. Rod grasped the silver fabric and flapped vigorously. "Come on!" he urged them. "You're not moving fast enough!"

He glanced down the road. No one was coming yet. I wonder how far away the roadblocks are, Rod thought, knowing that even during the winter there was normally local traffic between Santa Fe and the string of ghost towns to the south. Now the road was deserted. They were isolated and maybe trapped. A trio of blue spruce stood close to the west edge of the highway, their triangular silhouettes drawn darkly on the asphalt by afternoon sun. He looked at his watch again.

Ted grabbed his elbow. "Who rides in the *Windfoal*, Rod?" he asked. "Do you want me to fly it?"

"Yes, I do." Rod looked at the seven people remaining on the ground. "Take the archbishop and Mercedes. And hurry up!"

"But how are you going to—"

"Don't worry about it! Get going!" He pushed Ted toward the balloon. "Come on, Your Excellency. You too, Mercedes. Get in here as fast as you can!"

After they clambered in, and the *Windfoal* was hovering just off the blacktop, he spun around and dashed over to the little group working together to raise the last balloon. Joe had the fan at the *Sun Power*'s mouth now, and the governor and Serefina were waiting anxiously.

"Rod," she whispered the moment he reached her side, "how are we all going to fit in this balloon?"

"Shh," he told her, "we're not."

The black eyes widened, and she grasped his arm.

"Now keep your cool, *querida*," he said. "Valencio and Joe will be with you, and all three of you know how to fly. Forget solar and use propane like the others."

"But Rod, what about you?" Her voice broke.

He flung away from her and yanked the fan out of Joe's hands. "Okay, everybody in!" he ordered. "Serefina! Valencio! Joe!"

In the silence that followed, a look passed between the two Indian men. Rod impatiently grabbed Joe by his tattered Levi jacket and jerked him toward the *Sun Power*. Joe whirled from his grasp, and the coil of rope around his shoulder swung crazily, striking Rod on the cheek.

Valencio quickly stepped between them.

"Me and Joe, we're not going in the balloon. You get in, Riley."

Rod shook his head violently. "*Por Dios!* You go! Those bastards after us are killers. Get in!" He broke off, frustrated. Valencio stood stubbornly with his feet apart.

"The governor and I will make a run for it on the ground," Rod said.

"Please, Rod," Serefina begged. "They'll track you in the snow. You won't have a chance."

"Me and Joe are staying," Valencio insisted.

"No," said Cortés, "you don't understand. With me up there everyone in the balloons will be sitting ducks."

"No matter where you are, Governor, the balloons are in danger until they're out of rifle range," Valencio said, "but on the ground, you'd be a sitting duck."

Cortés scowled. Before he could open his mouth, Valencio pointed to the governor's rag-bound feet. "With that ankle and those booties, you'd be a *dead* duck."

"He's right, Governor," Rod agreed. "Valencio and I will stay."

"This is no time for cheap dramatics," Valencio said severely. "Use your head for a change. Joe and I know this country—you don't. Besides," he said, brandishing a movie rifle, "we have weapons."

Rod saw Valencio also had a knife on his belt and a rolled blanket strapped on his back. His black eyes were flinty, the squint lines etched around them from fifty years of hunting these mountains. The old man was right. He was green compared to Valencio and Joe.

"Jesús!" Rod burst out. "Okay! But don't play games with these people. Don't try to stand them off. Run for your goddam lives. These are the state troopers, and I mean they're out to kill somebody here."

Rod swung a leg over the *Sun Power's* gondola and hauled himself in fast beside Serefina and Cortés. The other pilots were hugging the ground as best they could, but a bottom breeze jerked at the balloons. *Windfoal* and *Rainbow's End* bumped against each other and bounced apart.

The sound of horses' hoofs drummed through the hissing of the propane. "*Cristo Rey!*" Serefina gasped.

"Fire your burners!" Rod yelled. "Head for heaven!"

Around the bend of Highway 14 galloped four horsemen. A deafening roar of propane torches rocked the remote mountain area as the riders thundered closer. From the corner of his eye, Rod saw Valencio and Joe begin running along the highway where the snow had melted and footing was good. The crack of shots snapped Rod's attention back to the horsemen. Each one was firing a rifle. Bullets streaked past, whining dangerously. Rod blasted the burner, urging heat into the *Sun Power*.

The silver balloon, like a magic bubble, soared up and up.

The *Camelot* raced after it, scarlet cross of St. George brilliant in the late-afternoon sun. *Rainbow's End* and *Windfoal* rose in their wake, the ground falling away.

But bullets kept coming. Rod heard Lauren scream as wicker splintered off the side of her basket. The burners roared. As if the sun were pulling them on long threads, the balloons mounted the sky.

A shot pierced the silver fabric above them. Rod touched Serefina's trembling hand. "*No problema,*" he said. "They can blow a dozen holes in the envelope and she'd still fly."

"It's the propane tanks," Serefina said, white-faced. "If they hit one, we'll be blown to bits."

Rod looked down. The ground was far below them now, a toy forest with a tiny road twisting through it; near the yellow bus, small moving dots—the four horsemen.

They were out of rifle range! Rod felt the sweat trickling down his back and chest. How close they had come! How lucky they'd been! No direct hit on a tank, no propane explosion. No one had been wounded. Thank God!

"Rodriguez," Serefina breathed, "we're safe!"

Cortés stared venomously at the horsemen below. "*Desgraciados!*" he muttered, with a gesture of contempt.

The balloons had caught a high air current and were moving south from the place where the bus had stalled. Rod searched the ground for Valencio and Joe. He couldn't see either of them. But he could see the riders loping north along Highway 14 in the direction the Indian men had run. Jesus, how he wished their prop rifles were real weapons. Valencio, he thought, I hope your Earth Mother hides you well.

"What's that?" Cortés pointed. Below, in a muddy canyon, Rod saw a long black Lincoln. Two men in dark suits were digging beside its wheels. The balloons drifted over them silently. "Tourists," Serefina said. "They never learn."

Lauren's blonde head rose cautiously over the gondola rim of the *Rainbow's End*. "Okay, what now?" she asked.

Rod said, "Since the cops seem to be trying to kill us, we

have to get to where there are people. We know the people are with us. We can trust *them*."

"You mean Albuquerque?"

"No," Rod answered. "I'm the only one with an extra tank of fuel because I ran on solar going to the tipi village. But the rest of you are low. You have maybe another half hour at the most. We can't risk a forced landing somewhere out there in the empty desert."

"How about trying for Santa Fe?" the governor asked.

"Same problem," Rod said, "Too far. Our best bet is to see if we can find a wind that will carry us over to the interstate where there are people. We'll flag down a trucker and get him to CB for . . ."

Rod and Cortés looked at each other.

". . . not the troopers," Rod said. "But who can we call?"

"The whole state security force can't be crooked," Cortés said.

"Is the chief in on it, do you think?" Rod asked.

"I don't know. I have no reason to suspect him. He's unimaginative and goes strictly by the book, but he's always done his job."

"Would you trust him?" Rod persisted.

Cortés shrugged. "I might, but I don't know about the rest of them anymore. Bernie Martinez ranked pretty high in the force. If he was in on it, how many other cops were? No, I think we'd better contact the attorney general instead."

"You're sure of him?"

"He's my mother's cousin—*familia*."

"We've got to catch a wind that will get us over to the interstate before sundown," Rod said.

The balloons were high. The view was immense. They could see from the tip of the Sandias that thrust up from the desert floor near Albuquerque to the Sangre de Cristo mountain range north of Santa Fe, whose peaks turned deep rose during sunsets, and to Mount Taylor, crowned with snow on the western horizon. From the foothills beneath them, the

172

desert spread out, bisected by sixty miles of arrow-straight interstate connecting Albuquerque and Santa Fe. About ten miles north of where the balloons were flying, Highway 14 wound out of the foothills and joined the interstate.

"We'll have to fly north," Rod announced, "and hope to reach that place up there where the highways cross." Then Rod pointed toward Albuquerque. "See that power plant back there? Those cooling stacks are a balloonist's landmark. You can tell the wind direction at that level from the way the steam blows. We need to go low enough to get into that north current. We may have to ground hug to the intersection."

He pulled the ripcord, and the balloon began to descend slowly. The other balloons followed. A southerly wind continued to push at them.

"Let more air out! Get below this air current!" Rod shouted to the other pilots. He tugged on the ripcord again, and the *Sun Power* continued its descent.

Finally, at two hundred feet above the ground, a northern current nudged the balloons in the direction of Santa Fe, flying them above Highway 14 toward its intersection with the interstate freeway.

Cortés stared back along the mountain road. "I wonder where those goddamn killers are?"

"If they were close, we'd know it," Rod replied. "We're so low, we couldn't get out of rifle range before they'd knock us out of the sky. Hand me the binoculars," he said. He strained his eyes for a glimpse of the horsemen—or Valencio and Joe.

They glided above the forest in the slanting sun. The giant shadows of the balloons walked up and down the foothills, sometimes shortened on the side of a hill, sometimes stretched to the east. The sun lowered and the light grew more golden, like thickening honey.

Valencio ran on down Highway 14, Joe close behind. Their feet clopped on the frozen dirt shoulder almost as loudly as horses' hoofs. They ran swiftly toward a sign that said, CAMPGROUND 2 MILES. An arrow on the sign pointed to a dirt road that turned east off Highway 14. Valencio trotted off the blacktop onto the campground road, gesturing Joe to one side of him. They ran abreast of each other, deliberately leaving two sets of tracks in the snow. Now their footsteps were muffled; the coil of rope and cartridge belts slapping against their jackets made the only noise.

The sun slanted west, sending long rays into the trees. The road ran between two low hills, and Valencio motioned with his head that they should continue.

When the road curved, Valencio stopped. Pointing silently, he sent Joe to the right of the road and he turned to the left.

Valencio moved quickly back into the trees and back-tracked along beside the road, as he knew Joe was doing on the other side. At the low place in the road, he climbed a small hill and waited for Joe. Soon his nephew appeared, scrambling through the spruce that grew on the opposite hill. Joe swung the end of the rope around and around and tossed it toward Valencio. His uncle caught the rope and snubbed his end around a sturdy tree, as Joe was doing on his side of the road.

When Valencio had finished, he eyed the rope critically. It lay slack across the road, hidden in the loose snow. It was barely noticeable, especially through the heavily plowed tracks he and Joe had made. Valencio ran his gnarled brown fingers over the loops of rope around the thick tree. Perfect, easy to pull taut as a bowstring at the right moment. If that didn't work, the sound of the prop rifles might hold the horsemen back long enough for him and Joe to run into the rocky arroyo where their tracks could be obscured. But that was risky. Without enough lead time, he and Joe would be ridden down and slaughtered.

Valencio eased the rolled blanket from his back and carefully unrolled it. On the dark wool lay the war bonnet.

Valencio picked it up in both hands, raised it once to the west where the sun was entering the House of Darkness and set it on his head. Then he squatted calmly beside the tree, waiting for the drumming hoof beats.

As the horses turned off the asphalt, the riders' voices carried up to Valencio's hiding place. "Watch for tricks," one of them called. "Redskins never did fight fair. Got to hunt 'em like wolves," another answered. The voice of the man Valencio thought must be the leader snarled, "They haven't got a chance, I'm going to ram those fake guns up their assholes!"

So they knew—the prop rifles were useless now. Valencio put his down in the snow and laid his hands on the snubbed rope. He and Joe would have to pull as one, but if they succeeded, the rope would come taut at the horsemen's chest level.

Through the trees Valencio could see the riders loping along the snowy road, the leader on the roan intent. Suddenly the man pointed ahead and pulled the rifle out of his saddle scabbard.

"Yeah," said the lead rider. "Gonna have a little fun with the Injuns before we kill 'em." He spurred his horse to a gallop. The horsemen came on fast.

Rod noticed a solitary car traveling south on Highway 14 just north of the balloons. From the *Sun Power* he could plainly distinguish the two cherries on its roof—it was a police car. The black-and-white barreled along at tremendous speed, swerving recklessly at every turn in the road.

When it was a little way up the highway, the car screeched to a halt, skidding diagonally across the road. A man jumped out the driver's side and looked up at the balloons, shading his eyes with one hand. He began circling his other arm vigorously in the air, making large, beckoning gestures.

"Give me those binoculars," Cortés said. He grabbed the glasses from Rod and aimed them at the figure on the ground. "It's Chief Daggett!"

"Daggett, huh?" Rod said, taking the binoculars back from Cortés. He focused on the uniformed man leaning against the car. The man in blue reached into his pocket and brought out a cigar. Rod watched as he bit off the tip, spit it out, and then lit the stogie. "Maybe he's the one the riders radioed."

"I don't think so," Cortés said. "Daggett hasn't got enough brains to be mixed up in something like that. He can't be blamed for one or two bad apples in the barrel—"

"One or two?" Rod persisted. "I counted at least four. With rifles. And you said yourself, who knows how many other cops are in on it." Rod watched as Daggett beckoned. "What's he doing here, anyway?"

"Someone must have seen our balloons, *qué no*? Daggett's responsible for my personal safety, so he came himself. Come on, let's get down there. He can get help fast on his police radio."

"I don't like it," Rod said.

He looked down at the fuel gauge. The needle was in the danger zone, but the solar balloon had an extra tank that could be switched with the empty. *Rainbow's End*, *Windfoal*, and the *Camelot* didn't.

Rod felt Serefina and Cortés looking at him intently, waiting for his decision. Finally, he cupped his hands and called to the other three pilots: "Let's go down!"

The *Sun Power* began her leisurely descent. The other balloons moved gracefully toward the earth in a triangular formation just above him.

"It's over," Rod told Serefina regretfully, avoiding her eyes. "Daggett will have all of us taken into custody." Serefina leaned against him. He folded his arms around her and kissed the top of her head.

"This was inevitable, Rod," she reminded him. "We knew it from the beginning."

The four balloons continued their descent. All attention was focused on the man below. Rod watched curiously as Daggett leaned into the car. He was radioing someone.

Abruptly, Rod said, "I don't like it. Sorry, but we're going back upstairs." He fired the blast valve.

"Get back up!" Rod yelled to the other pilots.

Cortés turned on him. "What the hell d'ya think you're doing, Riley?"

"Taking my own sweet time," Rod muttered, studying Daggett through the glasses.

Daggett reached through the sedan window and yanked out a rifle.

"Go up!" Rod yelled. "Get out of range fast!"

The balloons soared as blast valves were turned on full.

"Riley, you *mal parido!*" Cortés cursed. Rod kept the binoculars focused on Daggett. Through the glasses he watched the chief swing his rifle skyward, zeroing in on the *Sun Power*. Horrified, Rod felt sweat beading his lip and noticed the smallest details: the smoldering tip of Daggett's cigar; a ballpoint pen in his shirt pocket; and a name carved into the stock of his rifle—EL JEFE. Then the barrel seemed to stare at Rod out of its single deadly socket.

Oh, God, he thought, here we are on a sky hook, helpless. No way for me to shield Serefina or the governor. But surely only a madman would shoot!

The first bullet sliced through the air. No! Oh, no! Rod's mind raced. There was no protection in the lightweight aluminum gondola, but he pulled Serefina back from the edge. "Get down," he said, "don't give him your head as a target!"

A deadly hail of bullets flew after the balloons like angry wasps. Rod saw Lauren's frightened face as she crouched in the gondola of the *Rainbow's End* below him. He looked up and saw Mercedes and the archbishop leaning out of the *Windfoal's* basket.

"Get down!" He gestured frantically. Then a bullet split rattan off the side of the gondola. Mercedes and the archbishop ducked. "Phwa-twaanng!" A shot pierced the corner of the *Sun Power's* aluminum gondola. They couldn't get up fast enough! Another shot! A yelp from Ted Findley. "Oh, God," Moira screamed. "Teddy, are you hurt?"

"No!" Ted yelled back. "Just grazed my foot."

Rod's heart hammered in his chest. No time to get high enough for safety—the stupid bastard was going to massacre them all! A shot tore through the air, nicking the superstructure, narrowly missing the propane line. Daggett was shoving another clip into the rifle.

Rid stared as the fuel-gauge needle dropped lower in the danger zone. The others had even less propane. The moment their tanks were empty and the heat gone, they'd start sinking. Daggett would slaughter them. God, no!

Suddenly a silver object flashed by Rod, turning over and over in the air, quickly followed by another. Rod looked up at the *Windfoal*. He saw the archbishop lob a third.

"Chile!" gasped Serefina. "Grandmother's chile verde—she always keeps several cans in her purse so she won't run out." Serefina began to giggle.

As Rod watched, the tin cans sped toward Daggett like tracers. The first hit the highway shoulder, impotently spraying up a small puff of gravel. The second hit the shoulder, too, but much closer to Daggett's car. The third struck the base of the windshield, shattering the glass in a spiderweb pattern.

A furious volley of shots retaliated. Moira began to scream hysterically. Rattan splintered from the *Camelot*, and two more holes appeared in the *Sun Power*'s aluminum gondola. Serefina jumped and cried in pain, clutching her arm. Blood seeped from between her fingers. Cortés caught her as she lurched forward, his face a mask of fury. By all that's holy, Rod swore between his teeth, I'll stop that monster! He ripped the full propane tank from the leather straps that held it in place.

He raised the heavy cylinder over his head and held it steady as they drifted closer to Daggett. He had to be certain, had to let go at the right second. He stared at Daggett and tried to gauge the distance and trajectory. Three more seconds, then he'd hurl the tank. One—a shot whined past. Two—Rod jerked back as if he'd been kicked in the head. He felt the tank grow weightless as it was taken from him, saw Cortés's arm in a final outward gesture, watched the tank fall away from the governor's hand, flashing silver as it spun over and over toward Daggett's car.

For Rod, the detonation of the tank was a silent blossoming of orange. The force of the explosion rocked the balloons. Pieces of car leaped violently upward, writhing crazily in a death dance before crashing back into the fire and smoke. Flames consumed flesh and metal.

Rod put his hand to his head and felt the sticky wetness of blood. Dizzy and nauseous, he squatted in the gondola as pain began pounding his head. Serefina knelt beside him trying to stop the bleeding from his scalp with her bandanna. His ears pulsed in the cottony silence. Like floats on a huge fishing line, the other three balloons bobbed along in a row.

Rod touched the long deep scratch on the side of his head. He knew then he'd been creased by a bullet, and it was the concussion that had deafened him. Serefina's lips moved soundlessly. Bright crimson stained the sleeve of her jacket. He hauled himself to his feet, head throbbing, and looked down. An oily black column of smoke rose from the wreckage of Daggett's car.

Rod helped Serefina stand up. To the west the sky glowed gold and scarlet. Long pennants of cloud streamed across the sunset. In the east a skinny moon peered over the mountains. Along the interstate car lights blinked on like votive candles.

One by one each pilot signaled that his propane was gone. The balloons began to lose altitude as the buoyant hot air cooled. Finally Rod's fuel gauge read empty, too. The *Sun Power* sank slowly earthward.

The ringing in his head began to break occasionally. He dimly heard voices from the nearby balloons.

Suddenly he could hear galloping hoofs. In the failing light, he saw four horses racing along Highway 14 below.

The balloons were barely fifty feet above the ground now. He was afraid none of them had enough altitude to reach the intersection before they touched down. Unless they could reach the interstate where the traffic offered some protection, the four horsemen would shoot them.

The horses thundered along, their grotesque shadows flowing far behind them. As they came closer, Rod saw two of the horses were mounted, two riderless. "*Caramba!*" he heard from Cortés. Exuberant war whoops split the air. Below, riding like demons, Valencio and Joe raised rifles in salute. Valencio's war bonnet streamed majestically behind him.

The balloons, twenty feet above the ground, neared the intersection. Horns were blowing. Serefina leaned over the railing of the gondola, her dark hair swinging free. Traffic clustered along the interstate as drivers spotted the balloons. Semis tooted air horns: passenger cars beeped and blinked their headlights. Rod could see the balloons would be no more than five or six feet above ground crossing the interstate. Cars were no danger at that height, but any of them could be wiped out by a truck. He waved his arms wildly at the truckers. One of the truck drivers waved back and spoke into his CB. Soon most of the cars pulled over along the shoulder and the truckers filled both lanes, flashing emergency lights and rolling along slowly enough to allow the balloons to pass safely across the interstate in front of them.

Where the highways crossed, Rod could see cars pulling off into the sagebrush. People were getting out of the cars. "They're calling each other on CBs!" Cortés laughed.

Rod put his arms around Serefina. "Rodriguez, can you hear me now?" He nodded, though sounds still faded in and out as if he were listening to a seashell.

"Are you hurt badly?" Rod asked.

"I don't think so."

The *Camelot* was first down, skimming ten feet above the pavement and dropping abruptly on the other side. Lauren was more cautious with the *Rainbow's End,* and it sailed thirty feet beyond the freeway before landing smoothly. The *Windfoal* cleared the highway by less than four feet and landed on the shoulder.

Last to leave the skies was the *Sun Power.* The crowd of parked cars was now sizable and was growing as more cars pulled off the interstate. As the solar balloon drifted over them, a cheer broke from the people.

"*Cortés!*" yelled a hundred voices, "*Cortés! Cortés!*" The governor waved. Hats were thrown in the air. The cheering grew chaotic.

At last the *Sun Power* touched the sandy desert floor. Over his shoulder Rod could see the constellation of headlights. People began climbing through the barbed-wire fence beside the highway and surging over the sandhills toward the solar balloon.

They began chanting. In the dusk the sound was low, powerful as Indian drums, and seemed drawn up from the earth itself. "*No sunshine tax. No sunshine tax. No sunshine tax.*" Rod leaned on the gondola's rail, listening to the chant. He looked at Serefina. She was weeping silently.

Over by the highway, Moira clambered out of the *Camelot* and pushed her way through the crowd. "Teddy! Oh, Ted," she cried, struggling against the people surrounding the balloons. Ted waved to her from the *Windfoal.* "I'm fine!" he shouted.

A little beyond, Senator Claridge and Lauren helped Cliff out of the *Rainbow's End.* Cliff staggered toward the *Sun Power,* his good arm draped around Lauren's shoulders. Senator Claridge walked ahead, holding off the first of the people to reach them.

"Jesus," said Cliff, looking at Rod's bloody head. "You been to some war?"

"Nah," Rod answered. "I've been to a tea party—the war's yet to come."

He drew Serefina close against him and turned to Cortés.

"What now, Governor?" he asked. "What kind of charges do we have facing us?"

"Hell, Riley, I dunno. But I'm damn sure not going to do anything about them tonight." Cortés indicated the cheering people with both hands. "You can't jail a folk hero."

Above them, the sphere of the *Sun Power*, silver in the dusky winter sky, was a promise of summer moons to come. Toward them, over the hills, came the people of New Mexico to reclaim their governor and affirm their pledge that sunshine would be free to all.

EPILOGUE

Sunshine splashed through the window of the large room of St. Francis Hospital in Santa Fe.

The comfortable room overlooked the old world of La Villa Real de la Santa Fe, the Royal City of Holy Faith of St. Francis, legacy of the conquistadores and the prize at the end of the unholy Santa Fe Trail.

The spires of St. Francis Cathedral, where Mercedes had gone to hear the archbishop say mass, could be seen through the hospital window. Just off the nearby plaza was the flat roof of La Fonda, where Ted and Moira were staying after Ted's foot had been Band-Aided.

Beyond, narrow streets meandered crookedly around the squat adobe houses, the color of the earth that formed them. From kitchen windowsills, brave little geraniums in tin cans flashed coral and red. Several children were playing in one of the dirt yards below, now muddy from recent snow. The boys swung on a tire, one occasionally dangling an arm to scoop up a snowball from the shadowed areas under the old cottonwood. Winter was on its knees.

Inside, spring reigned. The hospital room was banked with flowers, bright clusters of daisies, roses, azaleas, and chrysanthemums in fancy plastic florists' pots. Stacks of letters and telegrams covered the bedside table, spilling over on to the bed where Rod sat propped against the pillows. His white bandage was wrapped at a rakish angle. Serefina sat quietly in the chair beside him, reading.

In the next bed, Cliff, sling on his arm and Stetson on his head, was playing cards with Lauren. He smiled broadly at the young nurse's aide in the tight uniform as she fussed with his pillows. Lauren rolled her eyes as the aide slowly walked out, hips rotating seductively under the strained white cloth, then laid down all her cards. "Gin," she said.

The door swung open, and two orderlies came into the room carrying a six-foot-high horseshoe made of red roses. The two pushed the enormous floral arrangement against the window, the only space available. It was three feet wide, and a battered feather war bonnet was draped across it, pinned in place by two arrows.

"There's a card," one of the orderlies said, and handed a small white envelope to Cliff.

Cliff tore it open. "Listen to this," he hooted. "It's signed by Joe. He says: 'Get well. Uncle and I are flying to Los Angeles to be on the Tonight Show.' "

Everyone exploded with laughter.

The young nurse's aide returned with a large waxed white box. She presented it to Cliff, pressing her thighs against the side of the bed.

He read the card aloud, raising one eyebrow, "Many thanks. George and Elizabeth Claridge."

Lauren swept the box from his hands and lifted the lid. It was filled with white orchids.

"I believe these are for me," she said smiling.

Cliff gave her a quizzical look. "Bouquets from a hostage? Next thing you know, Allan Blake's going to be sending you flowers."

"Hmmm, the commissioner. I'd forgotten all about him."

There was a knock at the door. The aide opened it. "Another visitor for you," she said breathlessly. "It's the

184

governor!" She giggled and straightened the skirt of her white uniform and stood at attention.

Cortés, elegant in an expensive gray business suit and handmade Italian shoes, strode past her. His face was determinedly stern. The room grew quiet suddenly.

"I see you've been agonizing over your fate," the governor said, eyeing the champagne bottles cooling in a bedpan full of crushed ice. "I've just come from the attorney general's office and I have news." He paused significantly.

"No charges," he announced. He shrugged his shoulders. "It's an election year."

Cliff whooped and threw his Stetson in the air with his good arm. Lauren caught the hat as Serefina took Rod's hand.

"Thank you, Governor," Rod said quietly. "I know you must have intervened—"

"*De nada*," the governor interrupted. "You saved my life back at the canyon. *Vida por vida.*

"Bernie Martinez was at my meeting with the attorney general," Cortés continued. "With Daggett dead, Bernie's even more willing to talk. Seems the police protection for the heroin pipeline came from the top. Daggett was running the show from inside the state security force. The only cops on the take were Chief Daggett, Bernie, and Daggett's four killers, Squad B. But from his position, Daggett could sidetrack investigations and arrests. It was a Mafia operation, all right, headquartered in New York. The AG is confident that once he gets Bernie's full story, he can destroy the entire heroin pipeline in New Mexico. With Bernie's testimony, Squad B will be in jail for years. Right now, they're in the prison infirmary; claim they fell off their horses."

"And the sunshine tax?" Rod asked.

"I've just called an emergency session of the legislature to convene tomorrow. No question that the sunshine tax will be repealed. The lieutenant governor made a last-ditch effort to talk me out of it. Betty still refuses to believe that the people can't be silenced."

"She won't be around after the election," Lauren said.

"Probably not," Cortés agreed. "Well," he bowed slightly, "should I say until next time?"

"I don't know about him," Cliff said, jerking his thumb at Rod, "but I'm going back to the Last Frontier."

"And I'm going to go back to playing with the sun," Rod said.

"Then I'm sure to be seeing you," Cortés said. "New Mexico is definitely going solar."

Cortés shook Cliff's hand. "Good-by, Mr. Randall, Mrs. Van Dressler." He took Rod's hand. "Mr. Riley." He held out his hand to Serefina and leaned forward and kissed her lightly on the cheek. "Glad your arm is better, Mrs. Riley," he said. "Until next time."

After he left, Cliff and Lauren went on with their card game and Serefina began reading again.

"I wonder just how long it will be until next time?" Rod said after a while.

"A long time," Cliff said. "Nobody's likely to forget the Sunshine Tax Hijack."

"People forget," Rod argued.

"Hell, Riley, you heard the man. It's an election year."

"But what about next year or the year after that?" Rod persisted. "Sunshine will be free, but they'll find something to tax in its place."

"Yep," said Cliff. He settled back into the pillows and pictured the sun on his adobe ranch house, the irrigated flatlands of the Last Frontier, the tribladed windmill that generated his electricity.

"Wind," he said finally. "Next thing they'll try to tax the wind."